SHIPBOARD RENDEZVOUS

"I'm terribly embarrassed about my eavesdropping," Paula said, and then they both laughed.

"It serves me right, though," she added, "for being so inquisitive that I get myself deeply involved."

"Are you sorry we have come together?" Louis asked.

"We're too old for shipboard romance."

"I am. You aren't."

They had reached one of the main staircases. It had a gold-coloured carpet, and on the walls were modern tapestries in navy blue and green and gold.

"My wife has breakfast in bed and a long lie-in in the mornings," said Louis. "I see they are serving a light breakfast in the bar by the Lido. Shall we meet there? Is seven-thirty too early?"

"I'll be there," promised Paula with a sense of having a plunge into something just as deep and alarming, in its way, as the waters of the North Atlantic Ocean.

ANNA CLARKE
CABIN 3033

CHARTER BOOKS, NEW YORK

CABIN 3033

A Charter Book / published by arrangement with
Doubleday, a division of
Bantam Doubleday Dell Publishing Group, Inc.

PRINTING HISTORY
Doubleday edition published 1986
Charter edition / October 1989

Charter Books are published by The Berkley Publishing Group,
200 Madison Avenue, New York, New York 10016.
The name "CHARTER" and the "C" logo
are trademarks belonging to Charter Communications, Inc.

PRINTED IN THE UNITED STATES OF AMERICA

10 9 8 7 6 5 4 3 2 1

1

Paula Glenning came into Cabin Number 3032 on the *Gloriana*, sat down on the dark green armchair, kicked off her shoes and lit a cigarette. The carpet was a lighter shade of green and the striped bedcover was a mixture of both. Over the bed was a curtain of the same material. Behind it was only a wall, but it gave the illusion of covering a window, and the big mirror over the dressing table increased the sense of space. Clamped to the wall opposite the mirror, and reflected in it, was a cool and elegant painting of arum lilies. A white-painted door led to the shower room, and another to a large clothes closet.

On the bed lay an open suitcase, half unpacked, and on the dressing table was a muddle of books and papers and clothes and toilet articles. Some of the contents of the suitcase had found their way onto the floor, but Paula made no move to pick them up. This was partly because she was by nature rather untidy; partly because she was feeling mildly depressed and disinclined to make any effort; and partly because, comfortable though the cabin was, it had the transient and impersonal air of a hotel room. The clutter of her own possessions gave her the illusion of feeling more at home.

But nevertheless she was too restless to sit still, and after a few puffs she stubbed out the cigarette in the ashtray, making quite sure that it was completely extinguished. In spite of her untidiness she was very conscientious about important matters, and what could be more important than fire precautions in a ship at sea. Then she hurriedly finished her unpacking, making space on the top of the dressing table for a few Bon Voyage cards and for a small leather folder containing two photographs. On one side was a snapshot of a family group against a background of sand and sea. Two toddlers were engrossed with their sand castle, and the sun-tanned parents stared at the camera, the man dark and stocky, the woman fair and slim.

Paula smiled as she looked at this snapshot, remembering the holiday in Cornwall when she had taken it, and feeling vaguely comforted, as she always did, by the thought of her sister Stella and her family. But when her eyes turned to the other snapshot her smile faded. It had been taken indoors, and it showed a man sitting in a deep brown armchair in front of a bookcase. He looked to be in his late thirties and had a thin, very intelligent face. This was Richard Grieve, author, broadcaster and literary critic. Paula was frowning because she was dreading the thought of meeting Richard again without being able to tell him with all her heart that she would marry him.

She cared for him very deeply, much more deeply than she had ever cared for her former husband, and to cause Richard hurt was unthinkable. The prospect of a life without Richard in it was almost equally unthinkable, and yet Paula felt something holding her back. She was no more able to come to a decision than she had been three weeks ago when she had left London. The American visit, happy and rewarding in so many ways, had done nothing to help her to make up her mind.

And she was now beginning to fear that a restful sea voyage was not going to help either. It had seemed an excellent plan, after a very busy three weeks, to travel back this way. It would surely give her a chance to digest her experiences and to work on the material she had collected for her book. Where else in the world could one achieve such total freedom from responsibility as on a ship at sea? No visitors, no phone calls, no duties or obligations; no shopping or cleaning, no meals to prepare. No distractions except those that one chose for oneself, and plenty of time to think.

Paula had been looking forward to the journey, but as soon as she had watched the last of downtown Manhattan fade away in the evening light she had begun to wonder whether it had not been a mistake. She had all the time in the world to be lazy or to get on with her writing: but she also had all the time in the world to worry about what she was going to say to Richard.

Up in the crowded dining room, where a buffet supper was being served this first evening at sea, Paula had found herself smiling brightly at a seemingly never-ending succession of strangers, and saying the same things over and over again, until at last the sense of being lonely in a crowd had oppressed her so much that she had hastily finished her meal and come down to her cabin to be at peace.

But it seemed that peace was not what she needed either. She felt even more lonely down here than among all those people upstairs. The thought flashed through her mind that it would be nice to be able to say "Good night" to somebody, and this was followed by an infantile longing to have somebody say "Good night" to her. Could she knock on the door of the cabin next to her own, Number 3033, and make some excuse to speak to its occupants?

Paula was quite seriously considering this possibility when a better idea struck her: she had come away from the dining room without waiting for coffee. Why not ring for some now? The cruise brochure stated that one could order anything at any time, and some of the people upstairs had been trying to think of outlandish requests. Paula wondered idly whether they had had any success as she waited for the night steward to come.

He was a thin, fair youth, pale from a life spent almost entirely on the lower decks without air or sunlight. He offered to pour out the coffee for her, and took a long time doing it.

"Are you very busy?" asked Paula.

"No, ma'am. Not in my department," he replied. "Not on the Transatlantics. It's mostly Americans, you see, ma'am. Now before this, we were doing an English cruise. Twenty-seven trays. Twenty-seven."

Paula took a moment to get the point of this remark, and then she laughed. "Oh, I see. You mean the English and their early morning tea."

"That's right, ma'am," said the young man in the blue uniform jacket, looking gratified by her reaction. Paula, who was always interested in people and inquisitive by nature, began to wonder about the private hopes and thoughts and dreams of this boy whose life must be in every way so very different from her own.

"What's your name?" she asked.

"Denis, ma'am. With only one 'n,' not two."

"The French spelling. But you're not French."

"Oh no, ma'am. My home's in Liverpool."

There was perhaps a faint trace of a Merseyside accent in the otherwise classless, place-less voice.

"Your folks live there?" prompted Paula, and was told that he had a mother, widowed, and a sister, divorced, who were always quarrelling but who nevertheless managed to run a small handicraft shop together; that Denis stayed with them twice a year for one week; and that he liked being on the ship because he met such interesting people.

"We've got Ramon Carrington, the film director, on this trip," he went on, "and one of the Scandinavian royal princesses. And there's also a famous pianist. Classical. I guess you'll be going to his concerts, being the highbrow type, if you'll excuse my saying so, ma'am.''

"I suppose you have made that deduction from all these books that I'm lugging around," said Paula. "Yes, I do teach at a college in London. But I'm afraid I'm nothing very grand. Not to be compared with your film stars and princesses. But surely you don't meet them yourself, do you, Denis? Wouldn't you have to be working upstairs in the staterooms and penthouse suites?''

"There's always ways and means," he replied mysteriously, and Paula had a sudden intriguing glimpse of the life that went on behind all those doors marked "Crew only" or "Private.''

"I guess you know everything that goes on in this ship, Denis," she said, smiling again. "I wonder if you can tell me anything about my next-door neighbours in Cabin 3033. I want to catch up on some sleep and I hope they aren't going to be noisy.''

"I don't think so, ma'am. It's a middle-aged couple. Well, she is middle-aged. Maybe he is a bit older.''

"Are they English?''

"She's English. I'm not so sure about him. He speaks very English but he doesn't look it. He looks clever, though. I believe he's a writer. Like yourself, ma'am.''

"Oh, Denis, I'm not a writer. I'm a college teacher who sometimes has articles published in learned journals, that's all. And I'm also one of those tiresome English people who likes early morning tea. Will half past seven be all right?''

"Certainly, ma'am. And if you fancy anything to eat or drink during the night, ma'am, just ring the bell.''

"Thank you, Denis. Good night then.''

"Good night, ma'am.''

And he departed with the tray.

Paula could not help liking the boy, even though he was

obviously a great gossip. She wondered how she herself was going to be described to anybody who happened to be interested in listening. But it was her own fault; she had encouraged him to talk, being rather a gossip herself, and she certainly felt much better for the little chat and quite ready to go to bed.

The restlessness and sense of malaise were gone, but she still found it difficult to get to sleep. The sea was calm, but the distant throb of the engines and the swish of the air-conditioning were disturbing, and then there were the mysterious creaking and whispering sounds that seemed to start up as soon as she switched off the light over the bed. Paula had never been on a long sea voyage before and the sounds were strange to her. Somebody had said, when she announced that she was going to treat herself to a slow and restful return to England instead of flying, that the 80,000-ton *Gloriana* was like an enormous floating luxury hotel and that you wouldn't even know you were at sea.

The first statement was true, but not the latter. In spite of all the thought and effort that had gone into making the passengers comfortable indeed, one did have very much the sense of being at sea, confined in this great luxury hotel for the next five days, at the mercy of one's fellow travellers and of the elements. A scene from a film about the *Titanic* flashed into Paula's mind and had to be quickly suppressed.

Gradually she became accustomed to the faint quivering of the great ship and to the sounds of power and movement. But just as she was dropping off to sleep at last Paula became conscious of quite a different sort of sound, a very human sound that was coming from the cabin next door.

Somebody was crying and sobbing, quietly and intermittently as if trying to stifle it, but obviously in considerable distress. Paula opened her eyes and became aware of a very faint chink of light at the corner of the wall behind her head. The partition was thin, and at this spot ill-fitting, so that the light filtered through from next door. She propped herself up on one elbow and listened more intently, but could hear no sound of voices or movement, nothing but the sobbing.

It was disconcerting and rather upsetting to know that only a few feet away from her there was somebody very unhappy. Had it been a radio or loud talking and laughing that was disturbing her, Paula would have knocked on the cabin door and asked them to be quiet, please, because she was trying to sleep. But one could hardly bang on the wall and yell at somebody to stop weeping. Besides, Paula was a soft-hearted creature and anything in distress—human, animal, or vegetable—acted on her like a magnet.

She would have liked to help. But this was a situation in which one could not help: one could only speculate. Presumably it was the middle-aged English wife of the slightly more than middle-aged and possibly not English husband who was lying weeping at 1 A.M. on this first night of the luxury liner's Atlantic crossing. Was the husband amusing himself with younger ladies at the cabaret show up in the lounge? Or enjoying a romantic moonlight stroll on the Boat Deck? Or had there recently been a quarrel, and was the wife trying to stifle her sobs because she didn't want the husband to know how hurt she was?

In that case it must have been an unusually quiet sort of quarrel, because Paula had heard nothing. Or else it must have taken place at the far end of the long cabin. Paula had caught a glimpse of the inside of another cabin, similar in position to Number 3033, with the porthole at the far end, and the clothes closet forming a sort of room divider halfway along. It was very spacious, and if in Cabin Number 3033 a quarrel had taken place at the porthole end, then not even an inquisitive neighbour would have overheard.

Paula's imagination, always active, began to picture the scene, and it was not until the sobbing had ceased and the various noises of the ship had quite lost their strangeness and actually become lulling to the senses that she fell asleep at last.

2

"So you are writing a book about G. E. Goff," said the little white-haired American woman who was sitting opposite Paula in the dining room. "How very interesting."

"I saw him once," said her husband. "It was the only time he ever came to the States and I'm sorry to say his lecture was very disappointing. Though maybe we ought not to expect great novelists to lecture as well as they write."

"But where are you collecting your material?" said the wife. "I didn't think there were any of the Goff Papers* remaining."

"Oh, I'm not writing about the great man himself," cried Paula. "There are lots of Goff scholars far better qualified than I am. I'm writing about his family, about his household. All the people who ministered to his wants and so made his writing possible. I've been visiting a former housekeeper of his who now lives in New Jersey with her son."

"Now that really is very interesting indeed," said the white-haired lady with markedly greater warmth than before. "I've always said that the people who look after the

---

* The story of the Goff Papers is told in *Last Judgement*.

geniuses—and most of them are women—have been neglected by scholars.''

"They used to be neglected," said Paula, "but not so much nowadays. Have you read that recent life of Emma Hardy?''

It then transpired that Paula's table mates, whose names were Eugene and Mercy Fordham, were both retired librarians. The subsequent lively discussion was brought to an end only by the arrival of the dining-room steward, who placed a menu in front of Paula and then retired to a discreet distance while she studied it.

"The smoked haddock is delicious," said Mercy. "I can recommend it.''

"Oh." Paula looked at the list of breakfast dishes with a mixture of horror and fascination. "But if I eat all that now, and in four hours' time there'll be an enormous lunch, and then afternoon tea, and then dinner—"

"You can spend the intervening hours in the health club and the gym," said Eugene. "That's what I propose to do.''

"It's all very well for you," retorted Paula, looking at the spare lean figure of the retired librarian.

"But you don't have cause to worry either, Paula," said Mercy. "You're young and slim. I'm the one who ought to be keeping right away from this dining table.''

"Would Madam care to order?''

The steward stepped forward. He was young and slight and very deft, but when Paula looked up at his smooth Chinese face she saw great weariness in the dark eyes, and the thought came into her mind that quite a large number of people were working very hard indeed to provide her and her fellow passengers with their lazy luxury.

She had a sudden impulse to tell the tired-looking steward that she, Paula Glenning, Ph.D., did not normally live in this style, but that she dwelt in an untidy little attic apartment in an old house in the least fashionable part of

Hampstead and worked very hard at trying to get her students through their exams.

The presence of her companions restrained her. "It's no use, I can't resist it," she said instead, and ordered grapefruit and haddock and croissants and honey. "My only hope is that it will get stormy and the sea will be rough and I'll be seasick."

The others laughed and they all three spoke at once, expressing their pleasure at being at the same table and wondering who would be occupying the fourth chair, now empty.

"A teenage all-night disco maniac," suggested Paula.

"A lazy lady who takes her breakfast in bed," said Mercy.

"A sensible sort of guy who eats two meals a day instead of four," contributed Eugene, and they laughed again, well pleased with each other.

"Will you excuse us now, Paula?" said Mercy presently. "We want to go to the library for a copy of the general knowledge quiz. It seems they have one every day. You have to hand in your solutions by two o'clock and there's a prize for whoever gets the most right answers."

"A bit of amusement for those of us who don't play Bingo," said Eugene. "Would you like to join us, Paula? We could form a syndicate."

"I think I'll leave it till tomorrow," replied Paula. "But if you are going to be at the lecture at half-past eleven, then perhaps I may see you there."

"Lecture? 'How to Choose the Right Hair Style for Your Personality,' " said Eugene, reading from his programme of the day's events. "Does that really interest you?"

And he glanced with a somewhat puzzled air at Paula's fair straight hair and clever pleasant face and at the comfortable-looking trousers and sweater.

"Good Lord, no," cried Paula. "I didn't even notice it. No, I meant the talk by the literary agent, Josephine

Black. It's in the Jacobean Bar, wherever that may be.
They can't be expecting a very large audience, or they'd
have had it in one of the theatres or lounges.''

"We'll certainly be there," promised Mercy. "Anything in the literary field, and we'll be there. But I don't
think we've ever heard of Josephine Black. Have we,
Gene?''

Her husband shook his head. "But I don't know many
British literary agents. Is she well known?''

"Not so much nowadays," said Paula, "but she used
to have quite a reputation at one time for discovering and
promoting new talent. Including her husband. Louis Hillman.''

The others looked blank.

"Haven't heard of him either?" Paula smiled. "No,
don't apologize. I'm much more ignorant when it comes
to modern American writers, and it shows how insular the
British are. Louis Hillman writes very English detective
stories. They are always set in the 1920s or 1930s and are
deliberate copies of the detective fiction of that period. I
don't expect they've attracted much attention in the States,
although they are quite widely read in Britain.''

"We've gotten a little lazy about reading reviews since
we retired," said Mercy, "but maybe the lady's lecture
will inspire us to read the Hillman books. Does he copy
different authors, or always the same one?''

"Oh, quite a variety of authors," replied Paula. "The
detectives are given different names, but it's not difficult
to guess the originals. They are not exactly parodies and
they are quite cleverly done, although rather laboured, as
one would expect. I've read two or three, and found them
good stories, but rather frustrating because I feel all the
time as if I should like to hear the author's authentic voice
instead of all these imitations.''

Mercy was interested. She had risen to her feet but remained standing by her chair listening to Paula. "It sounds

like somebody wearing a mask, or a series of masks,'' she said.

Eugene was becoming impatient. ''If we don't get to the library soon some wise guy is going to walk in ahead of us and finish that quiz first.''

''We'll talk later,'' said Mercy, smiling and waving a hand at Paula. ''See you at the lecture.''

Nice people, thought Paula, watching the Fordhams move away, Mercy trotting along with little steps to keep up with Eugene's longer stride. But after they were out of sight she experienced a sudden return of the depression that had attacked her the previous evening. The dining room, which extended the full width of the ship, was much too big for comfort. No hotel would ever have a dining room that size. One stared out at a sea of tables on the red carpet, and the tubs of indoor shrubs that were placed at regular intervals did very little to break up the expanse and ease the eye.

Paula sipped her coffee and watched the stewards in their lemon yellow jackets go back and forth to the serving area. They must walk miles at every meal, she thought, balancing those overladen trays, and if the sea is rough, it must be a feat of juggling.

''More coffee, madam?''

The tired-eyed Chinese boy was by her side again.

''Thank you,'' said Paula, wishing she could make some sort of human contact with him, but kept at bay by his invisible armour of politeness. Why should he be obliged to make conversation, though, she asked herself after he had moved away again to stand patiently at the neighbouring table, waiting for two large grey-haired American women to decide what they were going to eat; was it not enough that he should do his job efficiently and courteously?

Nevertheless she could not help wishing that her dining-room steward was as chatty as Denis, and was surprised at the fresh wave of loneliness that came over her. Since her divorce five years previously she had lived for the most part by herself, and was well used to eating alone, travelling alone, working alone. The need for human relationships was met by her sister's family and by many friends, both men and women, and some of them very close indeed. And if she were to marry Richard, that would end the lonely life completely.

Could it be the prospect of making such a commitment that was causing her present lowness of spirits, so unlike her usual self? Or was it the ship, so big and so full of strangers—and perhaps the very fact that she had no duties, no obligations, absolutely nothing to do except to be lazy and pampered? She ought, of course, to start working on those notes that she had made for the Goff book, or on the article about some modern American poets, but she felt at the same time too restless and too stale for any concentrated thinking. The sense of personal unhappiness behind the bright surface of jollity in this enclosed community simply would not leave her. Above all, she was haunted by the memory of that stifled sobbing in the cabin next to her own.

This morning she had got up early and heard no sound from Cabin 3033, but all the time she was showering and dressing Paula had been conscious of the proximity of other lives, and of an ever-growing desire to meet these people and learn something about them.

My curiosity is quite revolting, she said to herself as she got up from the table, but it was a comfort, all the same, to fix her thoughts upon some definite object. Pondering the best way to become acquainted with her neighbours, Paula left the dining room and wandered into the Midships Lounge, which was equally vast and also carpeted in red. At the far end was a dance floor and a platform for the band and the cabaret performers. Shining cream-coloured armchairs were grouped around the coffee tables, and the tubs with indoor plants were placed around the sides, making a sort of barrier between the lounge and the throughways.

A girl in a pale green overall was spraying water on the leaves of the shrubs; another girl was pushing a vacuum cleaner over the floor, and two young lads were emptying ashtrays. They seemed to be having some sort of an argument, which ended in laughter, and their Cockney voices were the only sign of life in the whole place. Paula was glad to get out of the lounge, with its stale, morning-after air. It needed people and noise and activity to be tolerable. Surely there must be somewhere on this ship, apart from the cabins, where one could go and sit within four walls and have at least the illusion of cosiness.

Perhaps the library. But first of all she must have some fresh air. At the far end of the lounge was a broad staircase leading both up and down. Hoping to find a way out to the open decks, Paula went up one flight and pushed at a glass door. On the other side of the door was a hairdresser and beauty salon, and beyond that was a long arcade of shops: a florist, a china and silverware shop; a jeweller, and shops containing every other conceivable variety of luxury goods. There were also drink and tobacco shops and a drugstore; a shop full of holiday clothes and another full of evening dresses. There was also, for the poorer members of the community among whom Paula felt she must class herself, a stationer's and a souvenir shop.

Paula strolled along, looking at the window displays and feeling that she had indeed lost her way. Up here on the higher levels one was not at all aware of the throbbing of the ship's engines or of the air-conditioning system, and there was nothing to be heard of the faint creaking and groaning sounds that had at first disturbed her in her cabin. She was walking along a broad, blue-carpeted corridor, with brightly lit shop windows on either side, and above was a white ceiling.

One had no consciousness, here, of being at sea, nor of there being any outside world at all. So overwhelming was this sense of soundless enclosure that Paula suffered a few moments of complete disorientation, even of panic. It was like being in a dream, a sort of padded, luxurious, air-conditioned nightmare, and it took all her powers of reason and self-control not to break into a run. She was pulled out of this state of mind by the sound of a pleasant, authoritative, disembodied male voice.

"This is your captain speaking. . . . At half-past ten there will be a lifeboat drill and we shall be grateful if all those passengers who embarked at New York will take part in the exercise. It is for your own safety and convenience. You will find life jackets in your staterooms, together with instructions for putting them on, and your cabin steward will be available to help you if you have any difficulty, and to show you the way to your nearest lifeboat station. At ten-thirty precisely the emergency signal will be sounded. This signal is as follows . . ."

Paula stood staring at a display of modern Wedgwood porcelain, half her mind taking note of the captain's instructions and the other half occupied with wondering why people who wanted such a dinner service should buy it on the *Gloriana* and not from the supplier nearest to their own home. But presumably somebody must buy these things, otherwise they would not be here. Supposedly there was a tax advantage, as with the drinks and cigarettes and tobacco, but the prices looked so enormous to Paula that she did not even want to speculate what they would be if not duty-free.

"Thank you, ladies and gentlemen," said the captain, "and I will take this opportunity of wishing you all a very happy cruise."

The voice clicked off and Paula glanced at her watch. There was an hour to go before the boat drill, which she was determined not to miss, largely because it seemed a

very sensible precaution, but partly because it might be
an opportunity of seeing and perhaps talking to the people
in the next cabin. She knew that they had come on board
at New York, and not at one of the earlier ports of call,
because their luggage had been delivered to the door at
the same time as her own. After the boat drill she would
go in search of the library, and then there was the lecture,
where she would meet the Fordhams again and perhaps
some other congenial people as well, and that would pass
the morning away.

I am obviously not intended to be a lady of leisure,
Paula thought as she turned away from the china shop and
tried to get her bearings. It might perhaps be a good idea
to go back to the Midships Lounge and start again. On the
other hand, having come so far, she was rather curious to
know where this wide corridor of shops led to.

As she hesitated, Paula saw a tall, sunburnt young
woman dressed in white shorts and a white shirt coming
towards her with a purposeful air.

"Hi," cried Paula, waving at her. "You look as if you
might know your way about. I've got a craving for some
fresh air and am trying to find a way out onto the Boat
Deck."

"Sorry," replied the other with a smile. "I'm lost too.
I am supposed to be playing shuffleboard with some people I met last night but I keep getting back to the Midships
Lounge. Do you think they make it so difficult in order to
keep the passengers occupied?"

"It's rather like the maze at Hampton Court," said
Paula. "I believe there are plans of the ship to be had
from the Entertainments Bureau, but since I've not been
able to find where that is either, it's not much help. What
happens at the far end of this corridor—where you've just
come from?"

"Elevators down to the lounge again," was the reply.
"I don't think it would help you."

They pondered for a moment.

"We could ask in one of the shops," suggested Paula. "Or do you feel that would be cheating?"

"It would rather," said the girl, smiling again. "Let's have one more try, and if we get lost again we give up and ask the woman in the souvenir shop to guide us. She's not so terrifying as the assistants in the other shops."

"All right," said Paula. "But that's always supposing," she said as they walked along side by side, "that we are still in a position to find the souvenir shop. I know it sounds idiotic, but I don't even know which way the ship is going and which end of it we are now walking towards."

"Neither do I. Here's another door. Is this the one you came through?"

Paula examined the glass door, which was narrower than those she had so far encountered. "I don't think so," she replied. "I came up by the hairdresser's. I never noticed this. Shall we try?"

"It's like *Alice in Wonderland*," said the girl as they went through the door together, finding themselves in a short corridor at the end of which, to their great relief, was a big window through which could be seen the dark line of the horizon.

"Nobody is going to believe me," said Paula, "when I tell them that I actually had difficulty in finding where the sea was. That looks like your deck games down there, and I've got a feeling that if I go up these stairs I might even get out onto the Boat Deck."

They smiled at each other and waved goodbye. She's nice, but I probably won't see her again, thought Paula. This really is a floating city, and I have to look on Cabin 3032 as my home. She pushed at a heavy steel door and came at last out into the open air. This was the freshness she had craved, but in fact she found herself gasping at the strength of the wind. People were jogging round the

deck, heads down, arms held close to their sides. Others
were leaning against the rail. Paula joined a group of the
latter, who smiled at her but did not speak.

It was cold as well as windy and Paula hugged herself
for warmth. She leaned over the railing and stared down
at the sea. It looked a very long way below, as if at the
bottom of a cliff, and the troubled, foaming waters were
racing past. Paula was amazed to see that the ship was
moving so fast and creating such disturbance in the ocean.

Not having a very good head for heights, she did not
look down for long, but raised her head and stared out-
wards towards the horizon. The water was a deep, deep
blue, broken here and there by the white crust of a wave,
and the sky was azure, brilliant with sunlight and without
a cloud to be seen.

The sense of vastness and openness, space and power
way beyond the control of feeble humanity was at first
exhilarating, but after a little while Paula began to shiver
from the buffeting of the wind and to feel hypnotized by
the endless line of the horizon. It was a relief to return to
the shelter of the carpeted corridor. She found her way
to the Entertainments Bureau at last, acquired a plan of the
Gloriana, and several leaflets giving advance notice of film
showings and other events. She returned to her cabin on
Three Deck with a sense of achievement and, even more
important, with a distinct sense of coming home.

3

The bed had been made, the carpet vacuumed, the ashtray emptied, and a neat pile made of her books and papers. In the shower room everything was clean and shining and there were fresh towels, a new bath mat, and sufficient supplies of soap and shampoo and tissues to last for several Atlantic crossings. The only thing that looked out of place was Paula herself, and she hastily washed her hands and combed her hair and decided that it would not, after all, take her so very long to get used to having nothing to worry about except what clothes to put on or whether she had the right eye shadow. It might be easier to be a lady of leisure than she had anticipated; it was certainly very agreeable to be waited on quickly and efficiently.

She took the life jacket off the high shelf in the clothes closet, put it on in accordance with the instructions, and took it off again because it was bulky and uncomfortable and it was still only ten minutes past ten. If she had been at home she would have thought: twenty minutes to spare, I've just got time to make that phone call or finish that chapter or write that short letter. But here, as a pampered guest, she simply thought that it was not worth starting anything for so short a time, and stretched herself out on the bed and picked up the day's programme of events, mentally taking note of those she wanted to attend, such

20

as the talk by the literary agent and the Scrabble Party and the classical concert and the country dancing, and those she would not mind attending, such as the handicraft class and the nature film. She rejected the talk on improving your golf, the invitation to find your partner for bridge, and the get-together for people travelling alone who wanted to make friends.

On the other hand, she thought, almost immediately reversing this last decision, it might be interesting to see what sort of people did go along to meet other people. Could they possibly have anything in common, any of them at all? And whatever would Richard, scholar and critic of formidable intellect and leading a life far removed from popular taste, think of the life on board this ship?

She glanced at the photograph on the dressing table and pondered this last query in a dispassionate manner, without any of the nagging doubt and distress that had assailed her when she last looked at the photo. It was as if her decision about Richard had been put into cold storage; as if life in the cocoon of the *Gloriana* was the only life that there was; as if nothing mattered except what took place on the ship. Friends and activities on both sides of the Atlantic belonged to quite another world.

I am becoming corrupted already, thought Paula; I am becoming completely lazy and irresponsible. But at least her sense of loneliness and malaise had gone. She yawned, switched on the radio, heard an American voice say, amidst much atmospherics, "The Soviets have responded to the recent peace initiative by . . ." and instantly switched the radio off again.

The world news was as irrelevant as her own personal life and must not be allowed to intrude into her cocoon. Besides, in a few minutes' time the emergency bells would sound, and she wanted to make sure that she actually saw her neighbours emerge from Cabin Number 3033.

Were they in there now? She could hear no sound. But

a moment later she heard footsteps and the click of a lock as a door was opened, and then, for the first time since they had left New York, she actually heard voices and could plainly make out what was said.

"Are you going to the boat drill?"

It was a woman's voice speaking.

"No," said a man's voice, calm and expressionless. "I've been through it all before."

"The much-travelled author." Paula thought she could detect a sneering note in the woman's voice.

"No more travelled than you are," said the man in the same deadpan manner. "Why don't you give the boat drill a miss and take a little more time to prepare for your lecture?"

Lecture? And Denis had said that the husband was a writer. Could it be that it was Josephine Black and Louis Hillman in Cabin Number 3033? A writer. And possibly not of English birth. Louis Hillman had been born Ludwig Bergmann, an easy name to Anglicize. Paula remembered having read this somewhere, although for the most part there was very little personal publicity about this author and he had, as far as she knew, never made any sort of public appearance or taken part in any radio broadcast. Paula had no idea whether he spoke with any sort of foreign accent. The man next door was speaking English perfectly; but Denis had said he was not English. Perhaps he spoke too perfectly for an Englishman. Denis was an acute observer; he would notice such things. But surely Denis would know that the woman next door was giving a lecture, even if it was only a rather minor item in the programme. Unless, of course, the young night steward was not quite so knowledgeable about the affairs of the ship as he wanted to appear.

All this went through Paula's mind in a flash as she shamelessly listened, holding her breath, and keeping her head close to the chink at the end of the partition.

The woman made a contemptuous sound. If I were writing about it I should have to describe it as a snort, thought Paula.

"My lecture," she said bitterly. "Big deal. Half a dozen half-asleep and overfed Middle Western couples looking for a bit of culture. That's what I'll get."

"You might have an interesting audience," said the man. "Quite a lot of people prefer to travel slowly and in comfort nowadays. And at least it's paying for our passage."

"Three decks down! Cabin 3033!" cried the woman, and her voice sounded so near the chink in the partition that it made Paula jump. "There was a time when I would have been offered a stateroom on the Boat Deck. And you would too, even now, if you'd only cooperate." The voice was now despairing. "You do it to spite me, Louis."

"I do not do it to spite you. You know perfectly well that I cannot and will not try to publicize myself in any way. We agreed on that from the very beginning."

So it is them, thought Paula. Josephine Black, literary agent who did a little writing and quite a lot of public speaking herself, and Louis Hillman, novelist, a professional couple who had achieved a fair measure of success but were now past their peak and in danger of slipping down that steep slope of no return into obscurity. They were not travelling as top V.I.P.s up amongst Denis' film directors and minor royalty, and Paula did not believe that either of them, even in their best years, would have come into that class. But they were nevertheless travelling in great comfort. If they were getting it free, or in return for one short talk by Josephine, then they were not doing so badly after all.

"We also agreed," said the woman whom Paula decided she must now think of as Josephine, "that you would take my advice on what to write. And also when to write it. Your last novel was published more than a year ago and you haven't even made a start on another. Do you call that keeping to our agreement? Do you expect me to support you in the style to which you have become accustomed without contributing anything yourself? If you don't produce something else soon people will forget your name and that will be the end of your career. Nobody is going to reprint your books or make film or television series out of them. You're not in that class of writer, Louis.''

The voice sounded bitter again. And nasty. Very nasty. But on the other hand there had been that weeping and sobbing at one in the morning. Paula could not decide which of the two to be sorry for. She waited for the man to reply, which he did after a short silence.

''That is our agreement and I am sorry to let you down. I have written nothing because I have nothing more of that nature to write. I'm finished, Jo. I'm never again going to be able to produce the sort of book you want. I've copied others for too long and if I ever write again it must be as myself.''

''Don't be silly. You can't write as yourself. You know you can't. Besides, you haven't got the talent.''

''How can we know that?'' For the first time there was emotion in the man's voice. Anger certainly, and perhaps also some despair. ''We've never tried to place any other kind of book.''

''If you're thinking of an autobiography—''

''I'm not thinking of an autobiography. I know that's out. All I'm thinking of is something with some original characters, some original ideas—''

''Original!'' cried Josephine. ''You don't know how to be original. It's that little bitch Veronica who's responsible for this. She's been pumping you up and telling you what a great writer you could be if only it weren't for me. And it's no good telling me that you never saw Veronica when I was giving that talk in Montreal, because I just don't believe—''

The next words were drowned out by an ear-splitting clanging of bells combined with a long blast of the ship's hooter. Paula gave a start and clapped her hands to her ears. She had been so absorbed in her eavesdropping that she had completely forgotten the boat drill. For one nightmarish second she had actually thought the alarm was real.

She got up off the bed, scrambled into her life jacket and tied the strings as securely as she could, and picked up her large shoulder bag, which contained her passport and travel tickets and money in addition to less essential objects. Then she stood hesitating. Wasn't there something else one was supposed to do? Oh yes. Put on warm clothing. But that would mean removing and replacing the bulky life jacket yet again, and suddenly she was tired of the whole business and wanted only to sit by herself and smoke a cigarette and think about what she had overheard. And after all, her sweater and trousers were fairly warm. In any case it was only a practice, and if ever, which God forbid, it was the real thing, then she hoped she would keep calm enough to remember what to do.

She opened the door, noticed that the door of Cabin 3033 was still closed, told herself that there was no need to linger now that she knew who its occupants were, and turned aside to follow the straggle of people who were making for the staircase.

"No, madam," she heard the stewardess say, "I'm afraid we must ask you to use the stairs and not the elevator. It would not be possible to use the elevators in an emergency."

But what of the heart cases, and the elderly or disabled people, of whom there seemed to be a fair number on the ship? Paula decided that it was best not to think of such things. This was not an emergency and there was not going to be an emergency. Not that sort, at any rate, although there seemed to be plenty of quite violent feelings around, and some of them very near her.

Up and up they climbed, and came to a halt at last in the wide lobby where the Entertainments Bureau and the card room were situated. It all looked very peaceful and bright and cheerful. It was hard to think of the area as Boat Station Number 5. Paula listened with less than half an ear to the young officer who was explaining the procedure for launching lifeboats.

So that was what lay behind the professional partnership of Josephine Black and Louis Hillman. She loved him—hence the sobbing—and she had held him for all these years because she possessed the key to his literary success. And he had chafed against her possessiveness more and more and had finally decided to try to break loose. And breaking loose to try to write something of his own would probably mean breaking loose from Josephine altogether, because she would never leave him space and peace enough to write in his own way. She might say she would, if that was the only way not to lose him, but she would not and could not do it, because he was her own creation.

It was very sad for them both, but Josephine ought to realize that there was nothing to be done about it but be generous and let him go his own way. Then, perhaps, in a different sort of gratitude, he might come back to her. This could happen, as Paula knew from her own experience, if one let go at the right moment and really stuck to the decision. But it was very difficult and very painful, and you needed an outside life, something quite apart from the man in question, if you were successfully to make the break.

Poor Josephine. It would be impossibly difficult for her, with both her feelings and her professional life so closely bound up with Louis. No wonder she was crying herself to sleep.

"That's cute," said a voice in Paula's ear, "getting the boats out through those big windows in the upper lounge."

Paula nodded and smiled and took a grip on herself and listened to the young naval officer for a minute or two.

"Does anybody want to ask any questions?" he was saying.

Yes, thought Paula: what happens to the weak and the disabled. But she kept quiet, because it was obviously not the time and place. People were making jokes now, loosening the inevitable slight sense of strain that had arisen during the young man's explanations. After all, they were here to enjoy themselves, and the sooner they could be done with disagreeable topics and return to their amusements the better. There are two sorts of crime on this ship, thought Paula: the first is to act in any way that might endanger the safety of passengers and crew; the second is to let it be seen that you are not having a good time.

Provided you don't break these laws then you can do anything you like—all the seven deadly sins are open to you. Lie in bed all day; eat to excess; drink yourself insensible; gamble all your money away in the casino; slander all those you envy; hate as much as you like; be too proud to speak at all. Adultery—of course. Commit murder? No. Perhaps not. That really would be going too far.

"Thank you for your cooperation, ladies and gentlemen," said the young officer. "In one minute's time the all-clear whistle will sound, but meanwhile I should like to remind you once more of what the captain said about lighted cigarette ends. It may seem that the best thing to do with them is throw them into the sea, but this is very dangerous. Please do not do this. The sea is a long way down and the chances are that the wind will blow the sparks to the side of the ship. There are plenty of ashtrays in every room. So please remember this. And also remember that the fire precautions on the *Gloriana* are the best in the world. Thank you again. Have a good day."

The whistles sounded and there was a rush for the elevator. Paula took off her life jacket and walked downstairs

with the more energetic members of the group. There had
been no sign of the occupants of Cabin 3033 at the boat
drill, and she noticed that the door was still closed. The
time was now eleven o'clock and at half-past eleven Josephine Black was scheduled to give her lecture. Half an
hour to recover from the scene that Paula had overheard
and to put on a public face. And this was after what had
probably been a sleepless night.

Paula began to feel sorry for Josephine. She could not
like her; neither what she had heard of her private self nor
her professional aspect. Josephine had acquired a reputation for bullying both authors and publishers and for getting her own way by somewhat devious means.
Nevertheless she was an unhappy woman. She loved, and
she was in danger of losing the object of her love. And
taking it very badly. Paula could not help but feel pity,
even while she wondered how the two of them were going
to resolve the crisis in their relationship.

It was shocking to eavesdrop and she would not go out
of her way to do so; but if it chanced that they started
talking again when at her end of their cabin while she was
lying on her bed, she would certainly not switch on her
radio or move away.

4

Josephine Black was a tall, well-built woman with close-cropped dark hair and large handsome features. Her audience filled the Jacobean Bar, a crescent-shaped area at the stern of the ship, panelled in dark oak, with chairs and cushions covered in a red and green scroll design on a cream background. There were more women than men present, and more middle-aged and elderly than young people.

"I am going to talk about the services provided to authors and publishers by literary agencies," began Josephine, "and I would ask those of you who know all this already to bear with me and to make your contributions to the discussion that I hope will follow this short talk."

Very competent, thought Paula; the best way to handle it when you know absolutely nothing about your audience. It was hard to equate the self-assured authoritative lecturer with the unhappy woman in the cabin next door. She glanced at Mercy Fordham, who was sitting next to her, and the latter gave a little nod, as if to confirm that Paula had been correct in her assessment of Josephine as a go-getter. Paula wished for a moment that she could tell Mercy what she had overheard, but of course this would be a far greater betrayal of Josephine than confirming the tough public image would be.

The talk was as brief and compact as promised and there was no shortage of questions. "Did the agent really read every word of every script submitted?" "Every manuscript received full and careful attention," replied Josephine. "What sized paper should be used?" "A4 was the preferred size nowadays." "How should one bind the pages together?" "Staple the pages of each chapter, or of each batch of, say, twenty pages, and put a loose light folder or an elastic band around the lot. This is easy for mailing and it is easier for the reader to handle small batches of pages at a time than to have to hold the entire manuscript."

"Do all literary agents charge fees for reading a manuscript?" was the next question.

"Most of them do not," was the reply, "although you ought, of course, to enclose the return postage. A fee is charged for editorial work done at the author's request, but this is returnable if the manuscript is accepted by a publisher."

It seemed as if the audience was made up of aspiring authors. Paula admired the courtesy and tact with which Josephine dealt with the questions. She would have liked to ask how Josephine herself would deal with an unknown writer who showed promise: where was the dividing line between "advice and encouragement" on the one hand, and "domination and exploitation" on the other. But this would certainly not be tactful, even though nobody in the audience save Paula herself suspected the true state of affairs between Josephine and her novelist husband.

The Fordhams were beginning to find the questions tedious. "Miss Black has already dealt with that point," said Eugene, when a fellow countrywoman of his began to ask in a rather roundabout way about agency fees.

Josephine smiled at him, but repeated her reply to the questioner. It seemed as if the session was now at an end. Several people were looking towards the bar, where two stewards were unobtrusively setting out glasses, when a fresh note was struck by a dark, bearded, youngish man who had come in late and sat on one of the barstools throughout the proceedings.

"Do you ever make any mistakes?" he asked. The voice had a faint Yorkshire accent and the manner had a hint of agression. "Do you ever, for example, refuse to handle a work which later enjoys success?"

"We all make mistakes," replied Josephine, and Paula thought she could detect some hesitation in the confident manner. "Literary agents are no more infallible than anybody else."

"Has it ever happened to you?"

"Many times." Josephine smiled again, having apparently recovered her poise. "Do you want me to list the occasions? I am perfectly willing to do so, but I have a feeling that time is running out and we ought to be vacating this bar and letting other people come in."

"I shan't be a moment," said the bearded man. "I'm only interested in one example. My own. You returned a manuscript to me once with some far from encouraging comments, and I thought I would take this opportunity of letting you know that I have been earning my living by my pen, or rather by my word processor, ever since. For the past eight years, in fact. That's all."

His moment of triumph, thought Paula, for which he has waited long. There was no mistaking the emotion in his voice as he spoke the last words.

"That's absolutely great," said Josephine with excessive brightness. "Your gain and my loss." And she beamed on them all, but Paula had the impression that it was a very great effort for her to do so, and that she was, in fact, not far from collapse.

"Thank you," said the bearded man, "although I doubt if you would approve of what I write."

There was a moment of uncomfortable silence. The au-

dience was restive, wanting to get to the bar for their pre-
lunch drinks. Josephine stood there straight and smiling,
but seemingly unable to speak the words that would bring
the meeting gracefully to an end. Mercy nudged Paula and
whispered: "Gene and I think somebody ought to thank
the speaker. Will you do it or shall we?"

"I'll do it," said Paula, and got to her feet, blaming
herself for not having done so before. She had formed a
sentence in her mind and was just about to speak it when
she heard a man's voice from behind her.

"I'm sure I shall be speaking for us all," it said with
the too-perfect intonation of one whose English is learned,
not native, "when I thank Miss Black most warmly for
her very clear exposition and for her most helpful and
patient replies to our questions."

Louis Hillman, thought Paula as she applauded with the
rest; I didn't even know he was here. Was this arranged
between them beforehand, or did he only come to the rescue when he saw her floundering? At least it showed concern for Josephine, even if he was looking elsewhere for
comfort and support.

"Who's that?" murmured Mercy in Paula's ear as they
got up from their chairs and the stewards hastily rearranged the floor space of the Jacobean Bar.

"I don't know," lied Paula. "Let's go and talk to Josephine. I felt sorry for her with that last question."

"Hell holds no fury like an author scorned," said
Eugene. "Do you know him, Paula?"

Paula shook her head. "I haven't the least idea who he
is."

"Let's go find out," said Mercy, and she hustled them
along to join the little group consisting of Josephine, her
husband, and the bearded man, who were moving slowly
across the lounge.

"We want to thank you personally," said Mercy, "for
a very interesting morning."

Introductions were made all round. Josephine and Louis both looked relieved at the interruption, but the bearded man, whose name was Colin Knight, did not look pleased.

"There's no need to pretend that you've heard of me," he said to Paula, who was trying to think of a tactful way of finding out what sort of writing he did. "You won't have heard of me. I'm not recognized in academic circles."

"But I don't only move in academic circles," said Paula. "I do move in other circles too." She had truly meant to be friendly, but her voice sounded patronizing and rather pompous to her even as she was speaking. Colin Knight seemed to have a gift for making people feel awkward, for putting them into a false position.

His features shifted into what was presumably intended as a smile as he replied: "The people you meet on this ship, for example. Not quite your type, are they?"

"I haven't got a type," retorted Paula, annoyed with herself for being unable to control her irritation, "and I've met some very pleasant people on this ship."

"Pleasant, pleasant. There's a portmanteau word for you. A blanket word. Covers everything. Says absolutely nothing at all."

This man is intolerable, thought Paula: he's like the very worst kind of student. Her curiosity about him began to give way to a longing to escape, and in despair she glanced at Mercy Fordham, who came over at once to release her.

"Now, Mr. Colin Knight," Mercy said, "I'm an old woman and I haven't any patience with mysteries. You opened up the subject yourself so you obviously want it followed up. What was this work of yours that Miss Black did not consider up to standard? Did somebody else take it on and handle it successfully? And what is it that you are writing now?"

Feeling confident that Mercy would tell her all about it later, Paula turned to Louis Hillman, who was standing by himself a little apart from where Eugene Fordham and Josephine were talking about the prices fetched at a recent antiquarian book sale.

"Mrs. Fordham tells me that you are working on a study of G. E. Goff's household," said Louis to Paula. "Would it be impertinent to ask what prompted you to undertake this?"

"Not at all," Paula replied. "I happen to know G. E. Goff's grandson, James, quite well. In fact we teach in the same Department of English Literature. And I also know Richard Grieve, who is probably the chief authority on G. E. Goff. They've both given me a great deal of help."

"I should have thought they would feel you were poaching on their preserves," said Louis with a smile. "You must have a very persuasive way with you."

"It's not a critical study of Goff's work," explained Paula for the umpteenth time. "I'm only concerned with his domestic life, so I'm not in competition with any of the Goff scholars. And the circumstances were rather unusual. But I don't want to bore you."

"You are not boring me in the least and I should like to hear more about it. Are you free after dinner this evening?"

"Well, yes. But your wife—will she be interested?"

"Josephine is going to a reception for those taking part in the entertainments programme. Shall we meet in the Jacobean Bar at nine o'clock?"

"I'll be there," promised Paula, then excused herself and ran to the nearest elevator. She got out at Three Deck and walked along the brown-carpeted corridor towards Cabin Number 3032 with the casual assurance of one who knows her way home.

"Well, Richard, my love," she addressed the photograph on the dressing table, "I sure have got myself into an interesting situation, as the Victorian novelists or Mercy Fordham might say. I aim to get acquainted with the wife and end up tête-à-tête with the husband. But Josephine need have no jealousy of me. Although he's really quite attractive. A sort of weary, greying air of distinction. And good manners. Though maybe this is all just as much of a fake as his novels. Does Josephine know what he's really like? What *is* he really like, this man who was born Ludwig Bergmann and has turned himself into a literary Englishman? Is the original buried forever, or does Josephine only hope that it is buried forever because she loves only her own creation?''

The sense of living in this other woman's life was again strong within Paula, and then, with the infinitesimal flickerings of thought and feeling, she was once more plunged into her own perplexities and had a disturbing impression of having glimpsed some facet of her own nature that she had never glimpsed before.

''Well at least Josephine does deeply care for somebody,'' she murmured aloud, ''and for that I could almost envy her. Could it be that I am not capable myself of any true and loyal loving?''

She stared at herself in the mirror and decided to make an appointment with the hairdresser. Normally she gave very little time and thought to her appearance, but in the closed community of this ship one's usual standards no longer applied, and appearances really mattered. In fact appearances were the only thing that did matter, not only physical appearance, but the account that one gave of oneself, the mask that one presented to this little world.

If you are travelling alone, thought Paula, studying the imperfections of her own face in the relentless strip lighting over the bathroom mirror, there is no reason why you should not put on a completely fake personality for the duration of the voyage. Nobody, except a few officials, even knows your name. I wonder if anybody ever does it deliberately? Josephine is herself, of course, because she is officially present. And Louis. And the Fordhams. Unless they are doing a double act.

No. Not the Fordhams. Paula smiled at her reflection and decided that she was, after all, wearing as well as any other thirty-five-year-old. Mercy and Eugene were so very much what they purported to be. International crooks or private persons seeking vengeance did not masquerade as retired librarians. Not on the *Gloriana*; only on a fictional Orient Express.

The Fordhams were all right. It was that uncomfortable little incident at the end of Josephine's talk that had started this disturbing train of thought. Colin Knight. A most offensive young man. Was he satisfied with his little revenge upon Josephine for that early rejection, or was he going to make a nuisance of himself throughout the voyage? Above all, was he going to attach himself to what Paula was already beginning to think of as ''her'' little group of literary acquaintances, and if so, how were they going to shake him off?

5

"Here she is!" cried Mercy. "Hurry up, Paula, and let me tell you the worst before it happens."

The Chinese steward handed Paula a menu. She ordered more or less at random and waited expectantly.

"Prepare yourself for the shock," said Mercy. "Colin Knight is our ghost table mate."

And she pointed dramatically at the empty chair.

Paula gave a squeal of horror.

"He didn't like the people he was sitting with," continued Mercy, "so he went to the office and asked to be relocated. There were only a few vacant places and this was one of them."

"I can't bear it," said Paula, seeing an end to all the comfortable chatty mealtimes. "What on earth are we to do?"

"I guess we make it so he doesn't like us either," said Eugene.

"But how?"

"We ignore him. Leave him out of the conversation."

"Could we do that?" Paula looked doubtful.

"Of course we can't do that, Gene," said Mercy. "We'll just have to eat our meals quickly and hope he'll always be late so we don't have to spend too long together."

She sounded irritable, and Paula guessed that the Fordhams had been having some difference of opinion over this before her own arrival.

"Where is he now?" she asked, hoping to avoid having to side with either husband or wife.

"In the bar," replied Eugene, "telling Louis Hillman what's wrong with his novels."

Paula glanced at Mercy, who nodded and said: "That's just about it. Poor Mr. Hillman is very patient."

"Who is Colin Knight anyway?" demanded Paula. "Did you find out what he writes?"

Mercy flung up her hands. "I had to admit defeat."

"The only time in her life," said her husband, laughing, "that she's not been able to prize out all the information she wanted."

Paula was disappointed, although she was glad to see that both Eugene and Mercy seemed to have recovered their equanimity. "Maybe he's not a writer at all," she suggested, "and he only said it to try to score off Josephine. Although somehow I've got a feeling it was true."

The others agreed. Paula's turkey salad was brought and she took up her knife and fork. "Let's not ignore him," she said cheerfully, glancing first at Mercy and then at Eugene. "Let's make a concerted attempt to find out what he writes."

Neither of them responded and for an unhappy moment Paula feared that she had offended them both, although she could not imagine why. And then she saw the reason for Mercy's turning her head aside and for Eugene's frown. It was not the Chinese steward who had come up silently behind Paula's chair as she was speaking: it was Colin Knight himself. He took the empty chair next to her and helped himself to a roll and butter before he said, breaking the embarrassed silence, "Is the concerted attempt to begin straightaway, or may I order my lunch first?"

There was nothing to be done but apologize and try to

laugh it off and hope that he had only overheard the second part of Paula's remark.

"All the same," she added, doing her best but conscious that she sounded arch and artificial and quite unlike her usual self, "if you don't tell us anything about yourself we shall begin to suspect that you are not a writer at all."

"You are suggesting that I am lying?"

It was said in a similar tone of voice, and there was no way to respond except in kind. Paula felt trapped in a sort of jokey enmity, the kind of relationship that can develop between people obliged to work together without liking each other. But in such cases one knew the measure of the game. Everybody understood that the silly backchat was a defence against giving way to open ill-will and that it would be kept within recognized limits.

But of Colin Knight Paula knew nothing at all, except that he seemed to have no other method of communicating with his fellow creatures and was determined, possibly through some sort of deep hurt or bitterness of his own, to make people dislike him. He even succeeded in provoking a slight change of expression, a barely perceptible aura of disdain, on the face of the Chinese steward.

"I'll have the Madras curry with rice, but you can forget about the chopsticks."

And he handed back the menu with the narrowing of the eyes and the twitching of the mouth above the dark beard that in anybody else would have been recognized as a smile.

"I shall have an orange sorbet," said Eugene Fordham as if making a pronouncement of great importance. "Or maybe just cheese and fruit. What's your choice, honey?"

"Oh. Fresh fruit, I guess," said Mercy, glancing at Paula.

"I'll join you," said Paula. "Those pears look good. My grandfather—he was a market gardener—used to say

that to eat a pear at its best you had to choose not only
the right day, but the right hour.''

"Is that so?'' exclaimed Eugene. "Well, yes. I guess it
is. Pears are always either too hard or too soft.''

"Not like apples,'' said Mercy. "I'm looking forward
to eating an English Cox. They ought to be ripe now. It's
my favourite apple.''

"I don't find them quite sharp enough,'' said Paula. "I
prefer the Granny Smith.''

Eugene then chipped in with his own preferences, and
the subject of apples lasted them for some time. It was
extraordinary, thought Paula, how the three of them had
each picked up the cue from the others, coming to the
undiscussed and unspoken but unanimous decision that
the best way to deal with Colin Knight was to keep the
conversation on the subject of food. And it was all the
more effective in that it sounded completely unrehearsed,
as indeed it was. They might well have been having just
such a conversation even if Colin had not been there.

It left him no opening for provocation. Even when
Mercy, perhaps feeling a little sorry for him, turned to
face him and said, "What's your favourite apple, Colin?''
he managed only to mutter that he didn't like any of them.
By this time Eugene was examining the cheeseboard, so
that a discussion of the cheeses of France, where the Fordhams were to spend several weeks, followed on naturally
enough.

Paula then told the steward that she would have her coffee in the lounge, not in the restaurant, and stood up and
included Colin in her goodbye smile. Five minutes later
Mercy joined her.

"Where's Eugene?'' asked Paula.

"Listening to Colin Knight's views on Henry James.
Now don't you feel sorry for him. It's his own fault. He
has very little patience and can be very quick-tempered,

but then he worries about being mean to somebody and feels he has to make amends.''

"I feel I've been mean to Colin too," said Paula. "Maybe he can't help being like that. Maybe he's having a nervous breakdown."

"Maybe. Then let him go spoil somebody else's cruise. Hi, steward!''

Mercy secured her coffee.

"I tell you one thing I've found out," she went on after the red-coated boy had pushed the trolley on to the next group of people, "Miss Josephine Black and Mr. Colin Knight are much better acquainted with each other than they are pretending to be. I noticed that after you'd gone and the rest of us were talking at the bar before lunch. I couldn't hear what they were saying, but they didn't look like people who'd only just met. I saw Josephine take hold of his arm and she seemed almost to be pleading with him, and he smiled in that nasty way he's got and shook her off."

"Did anybody else notice?" asked Paula.

"Gene didn't, but I guess Mr. Hillman did, because he stopped talking to Gene and said something to Colin about detective fiction and that set Colin off attacking Mr. Hillman's novels.''

"So Louis came to Josephine's rescue a second time," said Paula thoughtfully.

"Sure. Why not?" Mercy gave her a curious glance. "He's her husband. In like circumstances I'd expect Gene to get me off the hook. Which doesn't mean that we don't have our disagreements—is there a couple who does not?— but we've never failed each other in public. And if Louis Hillman's career depends on his wife's handling of it, then he'd better help her out when she's gotten into difficulties."

Paula agreed absentmindedly, which intensified Mercy's curiosity and started her wondering whether Paula knew

more about the people concerned than she was admitting.
Eugene had made no idle boast when he said his wife was
very good at ferreting out information. The outward appearance of the little white-haired lady was very deceptive. After some further talk, Paula felt herself in danger
of saying more than she wanted. She liked Mercy and was
hampered by her own desire to be friendly, but decided
that the safest thing was to invent an excuse to go away.

"I think I'll go and have a siesta," she said. "I didn't
sleep much last night and there's nothing on the programme this afternoon that particularly appeals to me."

"That's an excellent idea," said Mercy. "I'll probably
do the same. See you at dinner if not before. And the
concert this evening ought to be worth hearing."

"Oh. Is that this evening? Damn. I'm going to miss it."

Mercy did not ask why; it was Paula herself who felt
obliged to explain, although she would have preferred not
to.

"Louis Hillman asked me to have a drink with him. We
were talking about my work on G. E. Goff's household
and he seemed to be particularly interested in it."

Mercy laughed. "You bet he did. Take care, Paula. That
one has got a roving eye. I don't trust that English gentleman performance. Not one little bit. And our literary agent
friend could be very jealous. I don't trust her either. Any
more than I'd trust myself if you started flirting with Eugene."

"Me!" exclaimed Paula in amazement. "Do I look like
the sort of woman who goes around annexing other wom-
en's husbands?"

"Yes, my young friend, that's exactly what you do look
like. No, don't take offence," said Mercy, overriding Paula's protests. "It's a compliment. That's why we like you,
Gene and I. I don't say you do it intentionally, because
I'm quite sure you don't, and that's why it happens—just
because you're so unself-conscious and unaffected. You're

intelligent and kind-hearted and affectionate and sincere. That's a rare enough combination in itself, and if you add that to a lively manner and a pretty face, what more can you want? There aren't many men around who can see all that in their wives."

"I'm completely shattered," said Paula. "I've never seen myself as a femme fatale."

Mercy shook her head. "Not a femme fatale. Just a very nice true and loyal friend."

Paula, who had with some difficulty pulled herself up from the depths of the armchair, sat down again on the edge of it and faced the older woman.

"Listen, Mercy, I like you too, and I can't leave you, even for a little while, with such a very false impression of me. I'm careless and impulsive and inquisitive and my ex-husband found me impossible to live with because I'm hopelessly untidy about the house and I smoke too much. So if I can't even hold on to my own husband I really don't see how I can be the sort of woman who lures away other people's."

Mercy leaned forward and laid a hand over Paula's, which was gripping the arm of the chair rather too tightly.

"Forget it," she said very gently. "I'm sorry. You've had a painful time. I'm not probing into your affairs, Paula. But I'd like you to be happy. See you. Take care."

The last few words were spoken without any of the emotion that had filled the earlier ones. It might have been nothing more than the conventional American form of farewell.

"See you," said Paula, and she walked away across the red carpet between the groups of cream-coloured armchairs, very quickly as if she was late for an appointment, although in fact she had no purpose beyond that of finding somewhere to be alone and recover her composure.

Mercy's view of her had been very disturbing, all the more so because Paula felt that it had been spoken in

sincerity, and also in goodwill, by a shrewd observer. But
why, apart from the overall fact that people did seem to
behave rather oddly in this little closed community of a
ship, should a woman whom she had met for the first time
a few hours ago speak in such a manner? Could it con-
ceivably be that Mercy was warning her not to flirt with
Eugene? Of course not. The idea was absurd. There was
no doubt at all that Eugene adored his wife, and of the
two of them, Paula found Mercy much the more interesting. Perhaps it was best not to speculate, but to try to
forget the whole conversation.

The trouble was, Paula thought as she found herself
once more in the shopping arcade without any consciousness of having turned her steps in that direction, that if
somebody held a mirror in front of you that showed a facet
of yourself that you simply did not recognize, then it was
impossible not to think about it.

The sort of woman who appeals to husbands who are
disappointed in their wives. What nonsense. Richard isn't
discontented with his wife, she said to herself, once again
pausing to stare at the Wedgwood dinner service, with
its ghostly aura of butlers and parlourmaids and bored or
false faces above the stuffed shirts and the red finger-
nails. But Richard had once had a wife, and they had not
been happy together; and although Richard did not talk
very much about it, Paula knew that she was being constantly compared with Liz. It alarmed her to feel that she
was being given attributes that she did not think she possessed. All those qualities, in fact, that Mercy had just
listed.

How do they know that I am honest and loyal and affectionate and kind-hearted, she thought irritably. How do
they know that I am not cold-bloodedly and cynically ex-
ploiting other people's feelings towards me?

She took a few steps back in the direction from which

she had come, and stood at the window of one of the dress shops, staring at a glamorous tent-like creation in scarlet chiffon. I'd much rather be a femme fatale, she muttered angrily under her breath, instead of having to live up to this stupid girl-guide image. I can't possibly marry Richard, her thoughts rushed on; he's no idea what I'm really like; he thinks because we love each other we can find a middle way between my untidiness and his finickiness, but I know we can't, not permanently.

Barry had been just the same before she agreed to marry him. Paula could remember her exact words: "You don't know me at all. I'm a slut. I'm also rather bitchy." He had laughed indulgently, as if she had been confessing to nothing more serious than a passion for peppermint creams. "If I marry you, you'll regret it," she had said. They had both been very much in love, and this had carried them through a few years, but in the end he had thrown her very own words back at her, in a very different tone of voice.

The sort of woman whom other women's husbands believed they could be happy with.

The operative word was "believed." Was she always to be punished because they would not believe her when she tried to show that there was another side to her nature?

At any rate, she could not marry Richard. The decision was taken at last, not after a rational weighing up of pros and cons, but because of some remarks made by a stranger who would go out of her life forever when this voyage was over. But of course it was not Mercy who had tipped the balance. Paula knew now what she had known all along— she could not marry Richard. It ought to have brought some sense of relief to have made up her mind, but at this moment she could feel nothing except an almost intolerable sense of loss.

It was out of all proportion to the situation. They had agreed that they would remain friends or lovers or both and that their lives would continue very much as they were at present. So why should there be this terrible sense of blankness and hopelessness just because Paula would be keeping on her shabby little apartment in Hampstead and Richard his elegant flat in Bloomsbury?

"Excuse me," said an impatient voice in Paula's ear. She had not realized that she was blocking the entrance to the shop. She hastily stepped aside to make way for a tall, thin, and very expensively dressed woman who stared at her with such contempt that it shook Paula out of the dark cloud of her thoughts and spurred her on to seek a safer sanctuary.

Up on the Boat Deck the wind was still sharp, but at the stern of the ship there were some large screens giving shelter. Paula settled herself in a deck chair behind one of them. A few feet away sat two large elderly women wearing fur coats and head scarves. They were talking in Italian, both speaking at once for most of the time, and after the first glance they took no notice of Paula. The trickle of people walking or jogging past ignored all three of them.

Paula curled up in her deck chair, rested her cheek on her hands, and half-closed her eyes. She saw a blur of blue, half dark, half light, horizontally slashed by the lines of the ship's railing, which seemed to move up and down in a gentle, rhythmic motion that had a soothing and almost hypnotic effect.

I have not got to do anything or go anywhere for hours and hours, thought Paula: I haven't got to talk to anybody, and nobody knows or cares where I am. I have made a decision, but there is no need to act on it yet. In fact there is no possibility of acting on it, unless I use the ship's radio-telephone, and I am certainly not going to do that. I am imprisoned in this little world but at the same time I am free because nothing is expected of me. I am not going to analyze myself or anybody else. I am not going to think about anything.

The dark blue and the light blue were infinity. The line of the ship's railing moved up and down.

I am in limbo, said Paula to herself.

6

Six hours later Paula was sitting in the same deck chair.
She was wearing a warm coat over her short dinner dress
and had thrown a rug over her legs. The man sitting beside
her had done likewise. It was quiet up here in comparison
with the main deck, where cabaret shows were taking place
in the two large lounges. Nevertheless, there was quite a
variety of sounds. There was the night-time swishing and
splashing of wind and water, the distant throbbing of the
dance bands, and the creaking and groaning of the great
ship itself.

The different shades of blue had given way to varying
intensities of darkness. The ship's railing and deck were
lit up in silhouette, bringing to the two people sitting in
the shelter of the screen a sense of privacy that was at the
same time a sense of being exposed to view, as if they
were on the stage of a theatre. In the infinite darkness of
the night were the eyes of the audience.

"Are you warm enough?" asked Louis.

"Perfectly," Paula replied.

They had been talking for twenty minutes down in the
Jacobean Bar, not about Paula's work on G. E. Goff, but
about their impressions of life on the ship, and had been
driven by the constant pressure of people and the difficulty
of hearing what the other was saying to seek a quieter

spot. This, as Paula had already discovered, was probably the only luxury that the *Gloriana* did not provide.

The library, a comfortable little room in the centre of the ship, where one could borrow books or look at magazines or works of reference, or just sit and talk quietly, was now closed for the night. The card room, another peaceful haven, was filled with grim-faced bridge players. When they came to a similar sort of place, which was marked on the ship's plan as a writing room, they found it occupied by two lines of television screens, each one with its viewer and each showing a different picture.

"Video cassettes," muttered Louis, and Paula then suggested that they should try the Boat Deck.

"When I was up here this afternoon," she said after they had sat in silence for a while to recover from the noise downstairs, "I felt almost disembodied, as if I had no reality, as if I wasn't coming away from one place and travelling towards someplace else, but had gone right out of time. As if everything had become condensed into that one moment of experience. I'd been feeling worried and rather miserable beforehand, and then suddenly it was restful. Nothing mattered anymore. Do you know what I mean?"

Paula shifted slightly in her deck chair. She could see Louis fairly clearly in the light coming from the windows of the stateroom below. He was staring straight ahead and did not answer for some time, but there was no anxiety or tension in the waiting, only a sense of security and companionship.

At last he said: "I know exactly what you mean. Nearly fifty years ago I had a similar sensation while sitting on the Boat Deck of an ocean liner crossing the Atlantic."

Paula waited. Forty-five years ago. That would be shortly before the outbreak of the Second World War.

"I was sixteen," Louis said, "and had come to England with a small group of refugee children and young people. My father was German and my mother was Polish, both Jewish, and my home town was in what is now East Germany. The British authorities would not let us stay. There had been some bureaucratic muddle, but a religious charity came to the rescue and arranged for some of us to be transported to Canada. My mother had a cousin in Manitoba who had promised to take me in provided I made myself useful in the business, which was that of furrier.''

Again he paused, but this time for only a moment as if to select the best words for continuing the story.

"We were taken from the old army camp near Dover where we had been living, and put on a bus with our two small suitcases each, and then put on a ship going to Montreal. That was all I saw of England until ten years later. The Nissen hut near Dover and the bus journey.''

"Nonstop?'' said Paula, sensing that he needed a little prompting at this point.

"Not entirely. We stopped on the seafront at Brighton to allow us to answer the call of nature, but we were strictly forbidden to wander further than the public lavatory or to try to talk to anybody. A pity.'' He sounded amused now. "We rather liked the look of Brighton, but we were very frightened and very obedient. And none of us could speak more than a few words of English, so we could scarcely have got very far even if some of us had decided we would prefer to take our chance as Dickensian vagabond children rather than be shipped off to Canada.''

His voice was still light and detached, but Paula suddenly felt weak and sick with compassion.

"It was not one of the famous ships,'' he went on, "but it was perfectly comfortable and we slept four to a cabin. But I had never been on a ship before except on the short crossing from Ostend to Dover, and the North Atlantic was doing its worst and I was violently seasick.''

"And heartsick and homesick too,'' murmured Paula.

"Yes,'' he said in a matter-of-fact way. "My parents

had been killed, and apart from a friendship I had formed
with a boy of my own age in our group, all my contacts
with my fellow creatures were of what one might call a
business nature. Henry was even more ill than I, and was
only just able to carry off his belongings when the ship
reached Montreal, where, you will be glad to hear, we
were immediately taken to a large house belonging to the
charity in question and made very welcome and fussed
over by some middle-aged Canadian ladies for the next
few days.''

"You are right," said Paula. "I am very glad to hear
it. What about the experience on the Boat Deck?''

"Hardly an experience. More a mood. A form of existence. I've written the whole story, you know, and can
remember every word of what I wrote. Do you really want
me to repeat this section of it? It will take several minutes.''

"I should very much like to hear you speak it," said
Paula.

"All right. It's written in the third person, and the character is named Henry, after my friend. Here I start to
quote:

" 'When they came into the Gulf of the St. Lawrence
Henry was well enough to come out of the cabin and sit
in a deck chair, covered with a thick rug, because it was
at first very cold, and there was the bleak icy coast of
Labrador on the horizon; but later it was a bit warmer,
and they passed the island of Anticosti in the gulf and then
at last you could see both banks, so that it really felt as if
you were in a river, an enormous river.

" 'It felt strange to be alone up here on the Boat Deck
when most of the passengers were down below having
their dinner, but Henry didn't feel either lonely or unhappy. Many years later he was to find the right words for
the feeling he had then, in a poem by Emily Dickinson—

" '*After great pain, a formal feeling comes . . .*

" 'High up on that ocean liner, looking out at the far banks of the St. Lawrence River, he had the sense of having been through great danger and survived. He even felt that he could eat something at last, and the deck steward brought him tea and salad sandwiches, and they tasted better than food had ever tasted before.

" 'So he sat there and looked at the land, the blessed land at last, the new land. And when the river narrowed, he could see the banks more clearly; and sometimes they were green and there was what looked like houses on them, very small and far away; and sometimes they were red— a wonderful, flaming red, like a sunset against the blue sky.

" 'It was the maple trees, with their leaves turned bright red in the fall.

" 'Henry would have liked to sit there forever, dreamily looking, thirst and hunger satisfied, neither in one country nor in the other, everything else in the world forgotten; no grief, no fear, no love, no bitterness. No past, no future. No hope and no despair. Nothing but the great ship moving through the calm water and the flaming maple trees against the sky.' "

Louis paused. "That's the conclusion of that section," he said after a moment or two in his most expressionless voice.

"That was beautiful," said Paula. "When and where was it published?"

"It was never published. It has never been read by anybody except"—he paused for a moment—"myself. I never expected to tell any other human being of its existence."

"I don't know what to say," cried Paula after a troubled silence. "What do you want me to say?"

"There's no need for you to say anything. You are a scholar and a teacher of English literature and I value your opinion. It gives me pleasure to know that you like this little bit of writing."

"And the rest of it is similar?"

"I suppose so."

"Is it only in your head or have you still got a written copy?" demanded Paula.

"I still have a copy," replied Louis with reluctance.

"Where is it?"

"In the bottom drawer of my writing desk, buried under a pile of typing paper, in our house in Sussex."

"Thank heaven for that," said Paula. "I was afraid you were going to tell me about some horrific manuscript-burning scene, straight from an Ibsen play."

Louis laughed with what seemed like genuine amusement. "With Josephine as the destroyer? Oh no. She would never do anything like that. Respect for the written word outweighs all personal considerations when it comes to the crunch."

I believe Josephine has read this book, thought Paula; that is why he hesitated just now; and I believe that the nonpublication of this book is the source of the tension between them. Josephine does not want him to write in this way because it is his own way, not hers.

Aloud she said: "Would you trust me with the manuscript?"

"Why do you want it?" he asked suspiciously, even a trifle harshly.

"First of all because I'd like to read the whole thing, and secondly because I'd like to keep it safe for you."

"I don't believe you, Paula. I believe you want to obtain another opinion on it with a view to finding a publisher."

Paula had to admit that such a thought was in her mind. "And why not?" she continued defiantly. "If the rest of it is as good as the piece you've quoted then it ought to be published. In fact it ought to have been published years ago."

"Exactly. It ought to have been published years ago. Not this year or next. It's dead, it's out of date, it's of no

interest to anybody anymore. Stories of child refugees from
Nazi Germany—who on earth would want to read all that
old stuff? The world is full of homeless, homesick refugees. All over Africa. All over the Middle East. The Viet-
namese boat people. And so on ad infinitum. It's boring.
It's irrelevant. What a nuisance they are when they appear
on our television screens and in the advertisements of those
tiresome charities who still believe that it is possible to
shock comfortable human beings into giving of their sur-
plus wealth. No, Paula, it's finished. It's over. But I'm glad
I quoted you that little piece and I'm very glad that you
like it.''

''What I want to know,'' said Paula, ''and you'll think
I'm being interfering but I'm still going to ask, is whether
you were quoting your wife when you said that a book like
this would have no appeal nowadays.''

''I was not quoting Josephine,'' he replied, ''because I
have never asked her about it, but that probably would be
her professional opinion and I have to agree with it. Shall
we walk a little? It seems to be getting rather chilly.''

In silence they walked once round the Boat Deck.

''And what were you doing when you were fifteen or
sixteen years old?'' asked Louis as they came past the spot
where they had been sitting and started on the second
round.

''Trying to do better than anybody else in my 'O' level
exams,'' answered Paula, ''at a rather rigid and very com-
petitive girls' school in South London. I was very ambi-
tious and very cocky. My sister Stella was a much nicer
character.''

''Just the two of you?''

''Yes. Two little orphans. Our parents were killed in a
plane crash. I have no memories of them at all, and Stella
has very few. Our grandparents brought us up. They
worked very hard at growing fruit and vegetables for the
markets and they never understood why my father wasn't

content with the business, but took himself off to university on a scholarship and became a research chemist and married a woman from a much higher social class. And they were even more bewildered when I did much the same thing myself. It was just permissible for a boy to want to be a scholar but it was unheard of for a girl. We never actually quarrelled, but we drifted apart, and I felt rather sad and guilty when they died, within a few months of each other.''

Paula talked on. The rewards of her hard work; the wonderful years at Oxford; the first teaching job, the exhilaration of discovering that she really could communicate to others her own enthusiasm for great poetry and prose. It was doing her a lot of good to talk about the earlier part of her life to an apparently interested listener. It seemed to be restoring her to herself, reinforcing her own reality after the hours of self-judgment and hopelessness earlier in the day. She did not even notice that they were going the round of the deck for the third time.

''I ought not to have married,'' she went on. ''I'm not suited to it. I'm not adaptable enough.''

''You seem to me to be a very adaptable sort of person from the little I've seen of you,'' said Louis.

''People always think that,'' cried Paula with feeling, ''because I'm tolerant and easy-going. That makes them think they can change me into what they want me to be. They'd never try to do it with a rigid sort of person. They just take them or leave them. And they can't seem to see that it's equally difficult for a careless and impulsive and fluid sort of person to become more rigid. It's like water,'' she cried, suddenly stopping still and leaning on the ship's railing. ''Water flows all over the place. There's no rigidity in water. But it always finds its own level. You can't change its nature.''

''Perhaps,'' said Louis gently, ''you will find somebody who doesn't want you to change.''

"Perhaps," said Paula without much conviction, "but it doesn't seem likely."

She shivered. The night suddenly felt very cold. The wind and the waves and the darkness seemed to mock the tiny griefs and passions of these tiny mortal creatures.

"I must go in," said Paula. "I'm feeling terribly tired."

"We'll talk again tomorrow," he said, "and tomorrow and tomorrow—"

"And the tomorrow after that we'll be back in England. Which feels at this moment so impossibly far away that I can scarcely believe in its existence. But, Louis, listen. I've got to make a confession. If we're going to meet again, even if only for the rest of this voyage, I feel I've just got to tell you that when I was in my cabin this morning I could hear you and Josephine talking."

"What did you hear?" Again there was that touch of harshness, a slight slipping of the perfect English accent.

"I heard you telling her that you couldn't write any more of the type of novel with which you had made your name, and that you had to have the freedom to write as your own self, and she said you hadn't got it in you and couldn't do anything without her, but at the same time that she was sneering she also sounded very frightened at the prospect of losing you. And the previous night I had heard somebody crying and sobbing and trying not to be heard. It was Josephine, wasn't it, Louis, and not you?"

"It was not me." The voice was harsher than ever. "Englishmen don't indulge in such emotional outbursts. Not even in private."

"I'm sorry. I mean I'm glad it wasn't you." Paula sounded rather confused. "I mean I'm sorry for Josephine, but I do feel that you—"

She broke off, wondering what it was that she was really trying to say.

"Now I too must make a confession," he said, "since I hope very much that we are going to meet many times

in future. It was wrong of me to marry Josephine. I did it
for selfish reasons. I wanted to be a writer and she wanted
to help me. I like and admire her enormously but I have
never loved her and have not always been faithful. You
probably overheard something about that too. I'm not
making any excuses. She suffers a lot and the fact that I
try to help her in other ways does not make up for it. I
should like us to part, but not only would that be mon-
strous cruelty and ingratitude; there are other reasons too.
I am a coward at heart and am afraid of taking the risk.
But it gets more and more difficult to keep up the act. You
have come to a big decision on this ship and perhaps I
shall come to one too, but at the moment I can see nothing
but a blank wall and increasing unhappiness for both Josephine and myself.''

"I wish you would let me have that manuscript," said
Paula. "Surely you could publish it without consulting her,
and she would then have to face the fact that you are quite
a different sort of writer."

"I've told you. Nobody will want to publish it now. It
was written by a much younger self. If ever I manage to
write truthfully again it must be as I am at present, whatever that may be. Now comes the worst part of my confession. Josephine has a heart condition. She has driven
herself much too hard for many years. We keep quiet about
it and take what precautions we can. I do my best to pro-
tect her when she is under stress, but all the time I am
thinking that if only . . . Do I need to say what I am really
thinking? Does it shock you?''

"I suppose all of us at some time or other have wished
somebody dead," said Paula lightly. But nevertheless she
was disturbed by his words, because of the intensity of
longing and despair that lay behind them, the yearning of
the man for freedom of action and the yearning of the
writer for freedom of the mind. Poor Josephine. Poor
Louis. It did indeed seem a hopeless situation.

It was a relief to come through the heavy door and shut out the enormous darkness of the night. It was a further relief when Louis said that Josephine's party ought to be over soon and he would go and collect her from the captain's drawing room where it was taking place.

"And I'm going straight home to bed," said Paula. "At least it is quiet down on Three Deck."

"We'll try not to disturb you again."

"I'm terribly embarrassed about my eavesdropping," she said, and then they both laughed.

"It serves me right, though," she added, "for being so inquisitive that I get myself deeply involved."

"Are you sorry we have come together?"

"No. Not really. But where are we going?"

"Wherever you like."

"We're too old for shipboard romance."

"I am. You aren't."

They had reached one of the main staircases. It had a gold-coloured carpet, and on the walls were modern tapestries in navy blue and green and gold.

"Josephine has breakfast in bed and a long lie-in in the mornings," said Louis. "I see they are serving a light breakfast in the bar by the Lido. Shall we meet there? Is seven-thirty too early?"

"I'll be there," promised Paula with a sense of having a plunge into something just as deep and alarming, in its way, as the waters of the North Atlantic Ocean.

7

During the night a storm blew up and Paula awoke from a deep sleep to the sense of movement and the sound of something rattling. She switched on the bedside light and looked around the cabin, comforting herself with the sight of her own possessions and the now familiar green chair and carpet and the painting of arum lilies.

We are at sea, she said to herself; right out in the Atlantic, probably a thousand miles from any land, and the ship is rolling quite a lot in spite of the stabilizers, and that rattling noise is . . .

She listened carefully, then smiled to herself. It's not the skeleton in the cupboard; it's all those loose coat hangers on the rail in the clothes closet, the ones I don't need, knocking into each other as the ship swings from side to side.

She sat up in bed, very upright, testing her own balance. No, she did not feel in the least bit seasick; on the contrary, she felt rather hungry. Her watch said ten minutes past six, and she was to meet Louis in the Lido Bar at half-past seven, so there was no hurry. There was not a sound to be heard from next door. She wondered if Josephine was still sleeping. Then she remembered that at half-past seven Denis was to bring her morning tea and a moment later she remembered that it was not far off that

59

time now, because they were losing an hour every night, travelling eastwards, and she had forgotten to put her watch ahead an hour before she fell asleep the night before.

So instead of a leisurely shower she would have to rush. She ought really to ring for Denis and cancel the tea, but he probably wouldn't come immediately because he would be very busy with his trays, even if there weren't as many as twenty-seven of them. She was very much looking forward to being with Louis again because her mind was full of things she wanted to ask him and things she wanted to tell him; but just at this moment she would have been very glad to lie in bed and slowly drink some hot sweet tea, and then get washed and dressed equally slowly, because she had a suspicion that she might be feeling a little queasy after all.

She had put on her dressing gown and was sitting on the edge of the bed, accustoming herself to the rocking of the ship and feeling a little better, when the knock came at the door.

"Come in!" she cried, thinking that Denis was very early, which at any rate solved one of her problems. But there was no sound of the steward's key turning in the lock, and Paula got up and opened the door.

Louis was wearing light trousers and a dark blue sweater and he looked very tired, as if he had been up all night.

"Come in," said Paula, and then she lost her balance with a sudden violent movement of the ship and collapsed onto the bed. "Sorry," she said. "I don't think I'm seasick. I just seem to have forgotten how to walk."

"You need to anticipate the ship's roll," said Louis, "and if you are sitting or lying down you just go with it, but if you are standing up or walking you have to balance yourself against it. I got used to it on my first voyage back from Canada and I've never been ill since."

He did indeed seem to be remarkably good at remaining upright.

"I'm afraid Josephine is having a bad time," he went on. "She's been quite ill for the last few hours and I'd rather not leave her just yet. I'm sorry, Paula. I'd very much looked forward to our breakfast."

"So had I," said Paula. "There's lots of things I had wanted to ask you."

She spoke rather as if there was no question of making another assignation, but all the time she was thinking: if Josephine is seasick, and if the sea remains rough, and if I can keep well myself, and if Louis is a good sailor, which he certainly seems to be, then we can spend lots of time together.

There was another knock on the door and a moment later it was pushed open. With a skill worthy of a professional juggler, Denis inserted himself and the tea tray into the cabin, pulled out the flap from the dressing table, placed the tray on it, held it there for a few seconds, and said: "It's going to slide off any moment. It would be safer here. If you'll excuse me, please, ma'am . . ."

And with equal deftness he pushed aside some of the clutter on the dressing table and wedged the tray between a pile of books and the wall of the clothes closet. Then he let go of it at last, and stood back and surveyed it critically, his fair head cocked to one side.

"I guess that's okay, ma'am. Can you manage to pour out, or would you like me to do it for you?"

His blue eyes stared innocently at Paula; he appeared to be quite unaware that there was a third person in the room.

"I think I can manage, thanks, Denis," said Paula, suppressing a tendency to giggle, because she was beginning to feel as if she was taking part in some idiotic farce, but at the same time wishing that Louis would say something, and then again hoping that he would not. Even if he spoke

very quietly, as he had done up till now, it might be that
the steward's reply would be heard by Josephine on the
other side of the thin partition.

Louis said nothing until Denis was out of the cabin, and
then he joined the steward, held the cabin door slightly
open, and said in his normal voice: "My wife won't be
wanting breakfast, but I'd be grateful if you would bring
me some tea and rolls and butter, and some dry biscuits
and an extra cup."

"Certainly, sir. I'm sorry to hear Madam is not well. I
hope she will soon be better."

"Thank you, Denis."

Louis stepped back into the cabin and shut the door.
Paula was still trying not to laugh.

"In the bad old days when you had to fake evidence of
adultery in order to get your divorce," she said, "I guess
this would have been enough. Can't you just see Denis
enjoying himself in the witness box?"

Louis did not smile. "Did you have to go through that
sort of charade?"

"Oh no. They'd changed the law by then. Barry and I
had to sign various papers saying we'd agreed to part and
then pay our solicitors' bills. It was quite painless."

Paula glanced at Louis as she spoke. The expression on
his face made her feel ashamed of the offhand, throwaway
manner in which she had been talking and which had become second nature to her when speaking of her own affairs. She held to this manner even when talking to
Richard, with whom she had fewer pretences and defences
than with any other human being. But it seemed that when
boarding the *Gloriana* she had left her usual protective
covering behind. First Mercy Fordham, and now Louis
Hillman, had seen straight through to a whole area of
swallowed but undigested pain, but they were putting the
wrong interpretation on it and she felt she had to correct
the misapprehension.

"I am not still in love with Barry," she said, feeling sure that she was forestalling Louis' next question. "I was probably out of love with him even before he with me, and there have been others in my life since then, but it was very painful because all partings are painful and it was also like a personal failure, and that wouldn't matter so much if I felt I had learned from it and would do better in future. But the way I've been thinking and feeling and acting since coming onto this ship only reinforces that failure. It's not that I can't find the right person," she concluded, "it's that there is something lacking in me."

She had been speaking very rapidly, and stopped to get her breath.

"I'm sorry," she muttered. "I ought not to be talking like this and keeping you here when you want to be getting back to Josephine. I hope she's not been able to hear us talking."

"No, she won't have heard anything," he replied. "We changed round because she thought she might feel better if she was the other end of the cabin nearer the porthole. Of course we can't open it, but it seems to cheer her up a bit to see some daylight."

He stood up. The ship gave a lurch, but Louis still kept his balance. "Are you going up to breakfast?" he asked.

"I hope so," replied Paula. "I think I'll try to get to the dining room. It's rather a long walk to the Lido."

"In that case I'll come up in a couple of hours' time and look out for you in the Midships Lounge. The dining room end. Then you won't have many yards to stagger."

"And there's a ladies' room nearby, which is very important. I hope Josephine will soon be feeling better," Paula added rather belatedly.

"If she's not improved within the next hour," said Louis, "I'll call the hospital and get one of the nurses to come and have a look at her. But I will come up to the lounge, even if it's only for a few minutes. Take care. Hold on to the railing tight if you are going to walk upstairs.''

Paula promised to do so. After he had gone she experimented with the tea tray, successfully pouring out half a cup of tea and watching the liquid shift first to one side of the cup and then the other before she picked it up and drank.

After that she washed and dressed, which took up all her energy and attention, particularly while she was using the shower. Even when on land, with the floor of a shower room remaining horizontal, it was quite easy to slip on wet tiles or plastic and bruise oneself badly or even injure a limb. With the floor constantly tilting in first one direction and then the other, it was extremely difficult to keep any balance at all, and after bruising her arm quite painfully against the soap dish, Paula decided to abandon all bravado and simply sit down on the floor.

By continuing to take such precautions, clinging to whatever firm object was nearest to her, and spending as little time as possible trying to stand upright, she managed to get ready for the great adventure of going up to the dining room. Slowly and carefully she opened the cabin door. Here was another hazard: it was liable to swing either open or shut at any moment with a vicious crash.

It was just as well that she had taken such care not to emerge from the cabin with an uncontrolled rush because Denis was at this moment coming into the narrow passage that led to Cabins 3032 and 3033, doing one of his balancing acts with a tray, and there might have been a collision. Paula had an impulse to assure him that the little scene he had just witnessed was quite innocent, but hastily suppressed it, since it really was absurd to feel one had to explain oneself to the steward. In any case, Denis would believe exactly what he wanted to believe and would tell his cronies exactly what he wanted to tell them and there was no way to stop him. But it seemed as if the episode had done her no harm in his eyes, because he gave her a wide friendly smile, which very nearly included a wink, and said cheerfully: "There won't be many in the dining room this morning. Force eleven storm, that's what we're in. That's nearly a hurricane. Winds up to a hundred miles an hour. You name it. Lots of people are seasick."

"Doesn't that mean more work for you?" said Paula, feeling rather alarmed by this weather report but determined not to show it. "More trays, I mean."

"Not for me," he replied. "This is my last. I'm off-duty now. Going to bye-byes. Jenny will have to cope."

"Have a good sleep," said Paula.

"And a very good day to you, ma'am," he replied, composing his face before knocking on the door of Cabin 3033.

But she had only got as far as the main corridor when he was once more beside her.

"That was quick," she said.

"They didn't want me to help," he said. "Gentleman took the tray from me at the door. Very steady on his pins, he seems to be. He'd make a good officer. Looks all right for it, too."

And he gave Paula a mock salute and another wide grin and moved off with his easy swaying walk in the direction of the stewards' pantry. Paula thought it was really her own fault that Denis was getting a bit cheeky, since first of all she had encouraged him to gossip, and then she was discovered with a man in her cabin. But there was something likeable about the boy all the same, and she wished that he had actually gone right into Cabin 3033 to deliver the tray, because she would have liked to ask him how Josephine was.

It was not exactly that she suspected Louis of not speaking the truth. Why should not Josephine be ill, along with many others? Nevertheless there had been something in his manner that did not quite seem to fit the situation. It had been too leisurely, too unworried, with nothing furtive or guilty about it. As soon as she had decided this, Paula instantly found herself arguing in the opposite direction. There was nothing for Louis to be furtive or guilty about, and even if there had been, he had himself admitted that he had had affairs with other women and was presumably well versed in the art of keeping up appearances.

Josephine must be seasick, Paula said to herself as she reached the nearest staircase and began to climb, preferring to cling to the railing rather than venture into an elevator. What else could be the matter with her? Am I suspecting that Louis has drugged her so as to keep her out of the way? Nonsense. That sort of melodrama simply did not take place, not even on the *Gloriana* in a Force eleven gale in mid-Atlantic.

But she could not help wishing that Denis had gone into the cabin, and she even began to wonder whether she herself could think of an excuse for going in there to see Josephine. Surely there must be some sort of good neighbourly comfort that one could offer? Not food, obviously. Books? Flowers? Perhaps Louis would have something to suggest.

Mercy Fordham was sitting alone at the breakfast table. It was now well after half-past eight by the ship's time, but the dining room was almost empty. Groups of stewards stood around chatting, and every now and then one of them would rush forward to rescue a plate or some piece of cutlery that looked like it was slipping off a table onto the floor.

Even the chairs seemed none too secure. Paula clutched at the back of one of them for support as she crossed the floor space in front of her table, and they executed a little waltz, she and the chair, before regaining their balance in a momentary pause in the ship's rolling. At last, with a great sigh of relief, Paula achieved her own chair, and Mercy applauded warmly.

"The female of the species is much tougher than the male," she said. "Poor Gene has succumbed and has been feeling very sorry for himself. And I guess we'll be free of Colin Knight for this meal. What are you going to have?"

"Anything that's easy to hold on to and easy to eat. I'm afraid it sounds almost blasphemous in the circumstances, but actually I'm rather hungry."

The Chinese steward silently handed Paula a menu.

"Not cereal," she said. "I'll only spill the milk. Kippers—heavens, no! I love them but even in stable circumstances I can never cope with the bones."

"You could manage the sausages," said Mercy.

"Yes. All right. And coffee and lots of rolls. Thank you."

Paula smiled up at the steward as she returned the menu and was surprised to receive an answering smile. She remarked on this to Mercy after he had gone off to fulfil her order, and Mercy said: "It doesn't surprise me in the least. Scrooge himself would smile back if you beamed at him like that."

"Oh, Mercy, please!" cried Paula. "Be true to your name. I don't feel I can cope with any comments on my irresistible attractions this morning. I'm sorry about Eugene. Did you call the hospital? Apparently you can have an injection that sends you to sleep for several hours and you wake up cured of seasickness."

"He's had one. The nurse came round about an hour ago. A nice girl. Her name's Polly. I was going to call the hospital again and get her to come to your cabin if you hadn't arrived just then."

"That's very kind of you," said Paula warmly.

"You wouldn't have thought I was being interfering?"

"Oh no. I'd have been very glad of it if I had been ill. It's not much fun to be sick alone and with nobody knowing you are."

"Yesterday afternoon," said Mercy, "I was just a wee bit anxious after what I had said, and I would have apologized at dinnertime if we hadn't all been totally silenced by Colin. And by the time he had gone, you had disappeared as well."

Paula glanced up from her sausages and smiled at the round pink face under the neat white hair.

"You've got a mischievous look in your eye, Mercy Fordham," she said. "I guess I'm getting to know you a little. So you want to know how Louis and I made out last evening. Correct?"

"Quite correct."

"We had a very interesting talk—yes, just a talk—up on the Boat Deck. First about him and then about me."

Paula took a drink of coffee, which was quite a difficult operation with the ship rolling so much, and required concentration. It also gave her the chance to recollect what she had actually said to the Fordhams about Josephine and Louis, so that she neither contradicted herself nor gave away any more of the truth than was necessary to satisfy Mercy's curiosity. For Paula was learning to be a little devious. It did not come naturally to her but she was doing her best.

"It's rather what I suspected," she said when she had carefully replaced her coffee cup on the saucer. "Louis would like to branch out and try a different kind of writing, but Josephine doesn't want him to and thinks he ought to stick to the books that have proved profitable. He says he's sure she's right about the difficulties of changing style, but he'd still like to try."

"And did you encourage him?"

Trust Mercy, thought Paula, to hit on a question that could not be answered with a careful little measure of truth, but only with a response that would immediately reveal the degree of confidence that had been arrived at between Louis and herself.

"I suppose I did," she admitted.

"I thought so," said Mercy, and then added surprisingly: "I'd have done exactly the same in your place. But I never would have been in your place. Mr. Hillman would never be interested in confiding his secret ambitions to an old woman like me."

This time Paula did not rise to the bait and they accomplished some more coffee drinking in silence. Then Paula said: "Josephine is seasick too. They've got the cabin next to mine—did I tell you?—and when I was coming out this morning I ran into him asking the steward to bring some dry biscuits for her. He says she's been ill half the night and if she's not better soon he'll be calling the hospital."

"Josephine Black seasick," exclaimed Mercy. "It sounds unlikely. Maybe he's murdered her."

Paula laughed and then said thoughtfully: "I wonder if people ever do murder people on ocean liners. You'd think it would be simple, wouldn't you, to drug someone and then push them overboard to disappear forever in the waters of the Atlantic. The trouble is, from where do you push them? Somebody would be sure to notice if you tried it from the deck and it's no good from the cabin because you can't open the porthole."

"Not to mention the little matter of accounting for the disappearance," said a man's voice, "unless it was a stowaway who shouldn't have been there in the first place."

Colin Knight had once more come up noiselessly behind Paula's chair and overheard her words. She was both startled and angry and did not try to hide it.

"That's the second time you've done that," she snapped. "I wish you'd stop it."

"If you will tell me in what manner you wish me to announce my presence," he replied, "I will do my best to oblige."

It was said in his usual provocative way, but the effect

was rather spoilt by a lurch of the ship that obliged him to sit down very hurriedly.

"We'd been telling each other you must be seasick," said Mercy in a tolerably friendly voice.

"I'm never seasick. Where's our steward?" Colin gave his order in a somewhat less offensive manner than on the previous occasions, and then asked Mercy where her husband was. He muttered something that sounded like "Rotten luck" when she explained. It really looked as if he might be making a genuine effort to be more amiable, but it did not last for long.

"May I enquire whether it was any particular person who provoked this fascinating conversation about doing away with people on board ship?" he asked, looking first at Mercy and then at Paula. "You weren't, by any chance, referring to myself?"

The two women immediately looked at each other.

"I have inspired considerable animosity in my time," went on Colin, "which is inevitable when one holds strong views on any subject, but as far as I know nobody has yet plotted to murder me."

"You won't believe us when we tell you we were thinking of nobody in particular," said Mercy calmly.

"Nobody is ever thinking of nobody in particular. But I would guess, from the expressions on your faces, that I was not the object of your speculations. You dislike me, of course, and you are no doubt considering ways and means of getting rid of me, but they will be socially acceptable ways. Am I not right?"

Again Mercy and Paula exchanged glances. They had nearly finished their breakfast, and without saying a word, pushed back their chairs preparatory to getting to their feet. Another heavy lurch of the ship caused them to delay for a moment and in this slight pause Colin spoke again.

"Could it be that you were considering how to dispose of my highly respected mother?"

8

This time Paula and Mercy did not look at each other, but by unspoken consent they both remained seated, both of them hating to give Colin the satisfaction of creating a dramatic effect but unable to prevent it.

Mercy was the first to recover. "Okay. We'll bite. Your mother is on this ship. Have we met her?"

"You have indeed. Very much so. You didn't like her much. People seldom do. That's her tragedy. This bacon is undercooked. I suppose the storm is affecting the kitchens. Although I don't think the food is all that wonderful in general. Do you?"

"Josephine Black, I suppose," said Paula, ignoring Colin's last remark. "That would explain your disgusting behaviour at her lecture yesterday. Nobody is ever quite so offensive to a stranger. They save it for their nearest relations."

"Or for their recent acquaintances," said Colin, staring at her in a way that made Paula feel annoyed with herself for descending to his level. She resolved to try to emulate Mercy's self-control.

"Miss Black is your mother?" said Mercy.

Colin made a little bow over the table. "For my sins. Or for hers."

71

"I guess that means you are illegitimate," said Mercy briskly. "So Mr. Hillman is not your father?"

"Do I really look as if I am descended from that out-moded piece of Teutonic Jewry?" said Colin in his very nastiest voice.

"No," snapped Paula, goaded into breaking her resolution a minute after it had been formed. "You look like the product of a Glasgow slum."

She wished the silly remark unsaid the moment it had been spoken, because it was a slur on a fine city and because it would only please Colin to make her lose her temper. But he did not look pleased. On the contrary, he looked quite savage for a moment, as if he was having difficulty in maintaining his self-control. Perhaps in her thoughtless irritation she had hit on something near the truth.

Mercy came to the rescue. "You can't expect us not to want to know more, after such an announcement," she said to Colin, "but if you are going to amuse yourself by refusing to answer any questions, then we might as well go away at once."

She glanced at Paula, who took her cue and got to her feet. The two women made their way out of the dining room with as much dignity as was compatible with the need to clutch at each other or at the tables and chairs for support.

Just outside the entrance Mercy paused: "I've left my daily programme and my plan of the ship back there on the table. I'm going to fetch them. Don't wait for me, Paula. See you later."

"See you," said Paula, feeling quite sure that Mercy had done this on purpose, as an excuse for getting rid of her, because she wanted to tackle Colin on her own.

In her present mood Paula might have felt some resentment at this manoeuvre, but it happened to suit her to be on her own when Louis came up to the lounge.

He was waiting for her in an alcove near the dance floor, and apart from the crew members tidying up was the only human being in the whole vast area.

"How is she?" asked Paula at once.

"Much the same. I am going to get a nurse, but I didn't phone from the cabin in case she started saying she didn't want any medical attention. Josephine is not the best of patients. I shall go down to the hospital myself in a minute or two. How are you getting on? Did you eat your breakfast?"

"Yes, thanks. I seem to be getting my sea legs. But, Louis." She paused uncertainly.

"Sit down for a moment. Something's upset you. It's not just the storm. Was it something to do with our conversation last night?" he went on as Paula still did not reply.

"No, it's to do with something that Colin said at the breakfast table a minute ago. Is it true that he is Josephine's illegitimate son?"

"Yes. That's partly what is making her ill. He is always likely to turn up at inconvenient moments and make a nuisance of himself but it's the first time we've been stuck on the same ship with him."

There was a straightforwardness about this reply that Paula found reassuring and that dispelled some of the doubts that had been gathering in her mind about Louis himself.

"Who was his father?" she asked.

"An unsuccessful playwright. An alcoholic. Half-Scots, half-Irish. One of Josephine's few failures. He died about five years ago and since then Colin has used his father's name and has been plaguing his mother more and more. He's really rather a poor thing but there's no way to help him and nothing to be done except try to avoid him."

Paula digested this reply. "Did Colin really try to get

his mother to handle his manuscripts for him?'' she asked curiously.

''Yes,'' said Louis so shortly that she dared not pursue the subject. Then he smiled: ''I don't think it's exactly a day for the Boat Deck, do you? And if this storm goes on I suspect that some of the scheduled activities will have to be cancelled. Shall we meet for mid-morning coffee in the card room? There are so many people seasick that I'm sure we'll find a quiet corner to ourselves.''

Paula agreed. ''But I wish I could do something for Josephine,'' she added. ''I suppose she wouldn't like to be visited?''

''Not just yet,'' was the reply, ''although she might well be glad to see a different face later on. I'll let you know. It's kind of you to suggest it. So will you excuse me now, Paula? And please may I look at your plan of the ship. I seem to have mislaid my own.''

She handed it over. ''Keep it. I can get another. I think the hospital is on Four Deck.''

She smiled and waved her hand as he got up to go, but after he had gone she felt almost as restless and depressed as she had done when first boarding the ship and found it intolerable to be alone in this huge room that so much needed people and noise to make it feel alive. And yet when one really wanted a quiet corner on the *Gloriana* there seemed to be none to be found. It was very strange.

The day's programme, which Paula had brought upstairs with her, offered a lesson for beginners at bridge, a hairdressing demonstration, a talk by an investment adviser, and sundry other items, none of which particularly appealed to her. But there was also a reminder that the daily general knowledge quiz was available at the library, and this would be as good a way of killing time as any other. The Fordhams had won yesterday's prize, which had been quite an acceptable pen, and Paula decided to try for today's. With Eugene confined to the cabin, and Mercy hav-

ing what looked like a long conversation with Colin, the
main rivals were out of the way for the time being.

In fact there appeared to be only one other competitor,
a thin dark boy of about sixteen who was leafing through
one of the volumes of the Encyclopaedia Britannica. An
elderly woman was looking at a fashion magazine, and the
fourth person in the room, the librarian herself, apologized to Paula for having only just opened, although the
stated time was nine o'clock. She was a friendly, cheerful
girl, and she explained that this was her first trip on the
Gloriana.

"I thought I was a good sailor," she said, "or else I
would not have taken the job. But this morning—"

She smiled and shrugged.

"Are you feeling better now?" asked Paula.

"Not too bad. I guess I'll get through. There's not exactly a rush of customers."

The quiz this morning was a literary one, and Paula
filled in most of the items without difficulty. Reference
books supplied the answers to one or two more, and she
guessed the solution to the remaining question.

"That was quick work," said the librarian when Paula
handed in the form.

"I ought to have had a handicap," said Paula. "I actually teach English Literature."

The librarian, a South African who had studied for a
year in London, seemed pleased to chat. She was a great
admirer of G.E. Goff and became quite excited when Paula
told her that she was a personal friend of the grandson and
was at present working on a book about the family.

"The only one of the novels that I haven't read is *Last
Judgment,*" said the librarian. "I hoped there would be a
copy in this library, but there isn't."

"I'll lend you my paperback edition," said Paula. "It's
in my cabin. I'll drop it in later today."

They talked for a little longer, and when people came

in and Paula went away, she felt that she had spun another thread that bound her to her own everyday life. Such links with normality were very valuable, helping to counterbalance the feeling of having cut loose from all moorings, the sense of having lost some of her own identity that she had been experiencing since boarding the ship.

It was still rather too early to go to meet Louis, and she decided to go down to her cabin and fetch the book at once. And perhaps—although she tried to persuade herself that this had not influenced her action—she might have a chance to find out how Josephine was, perhaps from the stewardess or even from the nurse.

It was stupid and irrational, and probably only a reflection of her own uneasy state of mind, but Paula felt she would not be satisfied until she had either seen for herself, or heard it from a disinterested person, that Josephine was suffering from nothing more than the motion of the ship and her own personal problems. Vague apprehensions like this are usually quite unfounded, Paula told herself, but she could not help remembering that the last time she had had such a hunch it had been thoroughly justified, and the action she had tried to take on that occasion had done nothing to avert the tragedy.

In the elevator were three people from a table near her own, a worried-looking middle-aged woman and two teenage boys, who both looked very pale and miserable, and who pushed Paula roughly out of the way when they stopped at Three Deck so that they could get out first.

The mother apologized. "We're all feeling bad, and their dad is the worst of the lot. I do so hope the sea will soon calm down."

"I expect it will," said Paula, and hurried off along the corridor, feeling more in need of reassurance and comfort herself than qualified to dispense it to others.

There was no sign of life in the little side passage that led to Cabins 3032 and 3033. Paula opened her cabin door, switched on the light, found the paperback copy of *Last Judgment*, placed it with the other things that she intended to take when she went upstairs again, and sat down on her bed and listened to hear if there was any sound from next door.

There were only the noises of the ship—the engine hum, the swish of the air-conditioning, the creaking and groaning, somewhat heightened by the storm. It felt lonely down here: did Josephine feel lonely too? Or was she too ill to care?

I have got to find out how she is, decided Paula. I'll knock on the door; the worst that can happen is a snub.

But first of all she put her head close to the partition at the place where the faint chinks of light showed through at night. And then, listening intently, she thought she could distinguish, among all the sounds of the ship, the moaning of a human creature in distress.

It was enough. She jumped up and hurried to the door of Cabin 3033, banged on it and cried out: "It's Paula Glenning from next door. Are you all right? Can I help?"

As she spoke she was turning the handle and trying the door. At the same moment it was pulled open from inside. The ship heaved over, Paula fell into the cabin, remembered Louis' advice, and succeeded in regaining her balance. Josephine had fallen back onto the bed. It was not, as Paula had expected, placed against the partition that separated the two cabins, but alongside the large clothes closet that divided the room into two parts.

Paula took a few steps forward to make sure that there was nobody in the porthole end of the cabin, which was out of her line of vision, and then returned to Josephine, who was wearing a pale green dressing gown and whose face looked much the same colour.

"Excuse me," she muttered, got herself to her feet, and staggered across to the bathroom, which was to the right of the cabin door.

While she was gone, Paula looked around. The bed onto
which Josephine had fallen was made up, but the sheets
on the one near the porthole were creased and twisted. So
it was true that Josephine was sleeping at that end, furthest
away from Paula's cabin. Then why had she heard the
moaning? The obvious answer was that Josephine had been
making her painful way to the bathroom.

What else could be learned from this quick look around
the room? The furnishings were much the same as in Cabin
3032, but the picture on the wall was of white roses, the
little curtains either side of the porthole were green and
white, and there was a glimpse of a dark and angry sea
and dark grey sky to be seen through the gusts of spray
that beat against the thick glass.

The cabin was very tidy. There were no clothes lying
about, and the books on one of the tables lay in two neat
little piles next to a low bowl containing an arrangement
of red and pink roses, which was miraculously staying in
the same place in spite of the movement of the ship. On
another table lay a black document case, the lid of a port-
able typewriter, and the typewriter itself, open, and with
a sheet of paper wound round the platen. Paula leaned
over to see whether there was anything typed on it, and
found only one word: "Draft." Louis or Josephine? Either
of them could have been using it to make a draft of a letter
or some other document. It showed that one or the other
of them, or both, were of orderly habits, but gave no other
information.

The clothes closet was shut, and the only other signs of
personal occupation of the cabin was a collection of tele-
grams and greeting cards stuck to the wall near the porthole.

Feeling rather guilty, for she would have hated to think
anybody was snooping around her own cabin in this manner, Paula glanced at these, but they looked to be a very
ordinary collection of messages from friends and acquain-

tances. In any case surely nobody would stick something up on a wall in public view if it wasn't meant to be read.

Thus Paula was easing her conscience when Josephine emerged from the bathroom, letting the door slam noisily behind her, and moved unsteadily towards her bed. As she climbed awkwardly onto it, her dressing gown drooped to the floor and Paula saw something fall out of the pocket. She bent down and picked it up.

"I think this is your cabin key," she said. "Do you want it?"

"Yes." Josephine took the key from Paula and replaced it in the pocket of her gown before she added, "Thanks."

"Is there anything I can do for you?" asked Paula. "Or would you rather I went?"

"Don't go." Josephine stretched out a hand. Paula gripped it. The skin was hot and damp, the fingers clung to hers convulsively.

"I don't want any injections," said Josephine in a low voice. "No injections. I don't trust them."

"Nobody can make you have an antiseasickness injection if you don't want it," said Paula soothingly.

"Oh yes they can, oh yes they can."

"Would you like me to stay," suggested Paula, "and tell the nurse when she comes that you don't like injections?"

Though I don't know what Louis will think about my being in here, she added to herself: will he be angry? Is it possible that he really has got some plan to keep Josephine out of the way by some sort of harmless drug and that is why she is afraid? Or is everything just as it seems to be on the surface, that he really does conscientiously take care of her, including protecting her from Colin?

"Have you always disliked injections?" asked Paula, hoping to find out whether Josephine's agitation was due to a not uncommon phobia, or whether she genuinely thought she had reason to be afraid.

Josephine suddenly opened her eyes very wide. She stared up at Paula and said clearly and with great contempt: "You fool. Can't you see what's going on? You're being used as a cover-up. All he cares about is that little bitch Veronica."

Veronica again, thought Paula. I forgot to ask Louis who she is. Aloud she said: "I don't feel as if I am being used in any way at all. I had a very interesting talk with your husband last night and I am glad to have met him and to have met you too."

She was surprised to discover, as she was speaking, that this was perfectly true, and that she was just as interested in Josephine as she was in Louis. She was certainly not falling in love with him, although she was attracted to him and very fascinated by the apparently schizophrenic nature of his writing, and this human interest was helping her over a rather blank period. It was not Josephine's words that distressed her, but a further painful flash of self-understanding. She seemed to be getting into a habit of forming relationships to help her over rather blank periods, but never for keeps. "The sort of woman whom other women's husbands believe they could be happy with." Mercy Fordham's words came back to her mind yet again.

"So there's no need to worry about me or about yourself," she added brightly as Josephine, having apparently exhausted herself by her outburst, leaned back and shut her eyes.

Paula got up and went into the bathroom, dampened a sponge, and returned to wipe the sick woman's face. Then she straightened the bedclothes and rearranged the pillows to try to make her more comfortable. She was standing in the middle of the cabin, wondering whether there was anything else she could do, when the knock came at the door.

"I don't want an injection," said Josephine, feebly moving her hand. "Don't let them give me an injection."

"All right," said Paula. "If that's the nurse, I'll tell her."

Josephine responded with a moan, which Paula took to mean that the nausea was overcoming her again. She moved towards the door wondering why, if Louis had come back with the nurse, they had not come straight in without knocking. As she opened the door her mind was framing words to explain her own presence and to pass on Josephine's wishes.

Colin Knight stood in the doorway.

"The ubiquitous Dr. Glenning," he said. "I did not realize that you were a doctor of medicine as well as of philosophy."

"Your mother is feeling rather ill," said Paula calmly. "She isn't fit to have visitors."

"Then what are you doing here, may I ask?"

"Staying with her while Mr. Hillman tries to find a nurse who is free."

"Did he ask you to?"

"No, but she did," retorted Paula, glad to be able to speak the truth, for Josephine had indeed begged her to stay.

This silenced him for a second or two. Paula had some hope that she might be able to persuade him to go away, but unfortunately Josephine chose this moment to heave herself out of the bed and to stand clinging to the end of it, in full view of the door. Colin pushed past Paula and into the cabin.

"My God, Ma, you do look awful!" he cried. "Why on earth didn't you go by air as you usually do?"

"Because we got a free passage this way," shouted Josephine, "in return for my lecture, which you did your damnedest to ruin! And who has paid for your passage, I'd like to know? Me as usual, I suppose. With the money I gave you to print your pornographic paperbacks."

It was extraordinary, thought Paula, how the violent

emotion aroused by Colin's presence appeared to have cured Josephine's nausea, even if only temporarily.

"They're not pornographic paperbacks," Colin yelled back. "They're perfectly legal. They're marketed by respectable booksellers."

"Not enough to keep you in cigarettes," retorted Josephine. "Not enough to stop you sponging on me. But it's going to finish. Now. Pronto. Not another penny. Not another cent. I'm done with the lot of you. Louis refuses to write any more novels and wants to write something totally unsaleable so that he can prove he's a genius and you think you can live off the drivel you're producing and refuse to get a decent job. Do you think I'm made of money? Do you think I want to work eighteen hours a day to keep you lazing about?"

Paula, fascinated, and not feeling at all guilty about overhearing this family quarrel since neither of them seemed to mind in the least that she was present, stood leaning against the cabin door.

"Yes, Ma, that's just what I do think," said Colin in reply to Josephine's rhetorical question. "If ever there was a workaholic, that's you. And how you enjoy feeling your power over all those wretched authors! Never got your claws into me though, did you? What a lucky escape for me that was when you blasted to bits my poor little youthful efforts. Saved me from a life sentence. Not like poor old Louis. But I tell you what, Ma," added Colin, coming nearer to Josephine as she stood momentarily speechless, clinging to the handle of the clothes closet to keep her upright, "you'd better not drive him too far. One of these days the worm is going to turn and it might be a lot sooner than you think."

"Don't you dare say a word against Louis!" shouted Josephine. "If you'd worked half as hard as he does you wouldn't be scrounging off me now. I'm sick of it, I tell you. Sick, sick . . . Oh my God!"

She let go of the clothes closet and clapped her hands over her mouth and once more staggered into the bathroom.

Colin turned to Paula. "Did you find that interesting? You rather enjoy getting involved in other people's affairs, don't you?"

"I wish that nurse would come," said Paula. "Your mother could do with some medical attention and some peace and quiet."

"I do believe you are really concerned about her," said Colin, for once without sarcasm. "One tends to forget that there are people who actually admire my mother. I admit that she has been quite a formidable figure in her day, but she's past it, you know, losing her touch. Shows her personal feelings too much. Overdoes the bullying and the editorial interference but doesn't deliver the goods. The future best-sellers are going elsewhere. Poor old Josephine. If you're thinking of submitting your literary efforts to anybody I would strongly advise you to try a different agency."

"Just now," said Paula curtly, "I'm thinking of nothing but of getting some medical advice."

He could not immediately think of a suitable retort to this, and the next moment the long-awaited knock came on the door.

— 9 —

A fair young woman dressed in a white uniform came in and spoke to Paula.

"Mrs. Hillman?"

"She's in the bathroom," said Paula.

The nurse glanced around. She was about Paula's age, but rather taller. "I think," she said, addressing Colin, "it might be best if Mrs. Hillman doesn't have any visitors just now."

The voice was friendly enough, but firm, and Paula noticed the Canadian accent. Colin, rather to Paula's surprise, made no protest. "I'll come back later," he muttered, and left the cabin.

The nurse then looked at Paula, who said: "She seemed to be in some difficulty and I came in from the next-door cabin to see if I could help."

"Thank you," said the nurse. "That was kind of you."

Her tone was dismissive.

"There's just one thing," said Paula. "No, two things. Where is Mr. Hillman? Isn't he with you?"

"No. Should he be?"

"He said he was going to the hospital to fetch a nurse," said Paula rather feebly, "but it was quite a while ago."

"I don't know anything about that," replied the girl in her impersonal way. "I've been visiting several other pas-

sengers and when I got back to the reception desk I found
a message to come to Cabin 3033.''

Somehow this answer made Paula feel a little uneasy,
although there was no reason why Louis, finding no nurse
free, couldn't have simply left a message for one to come
as soon as available. But in that case why had he not returned to the cabin and remained there? Could it possibly
be that Josephine was right after all, and that he was taking
the opportunity to see Veronica, whoever she might be,
and possibly even standing Paula up in the process?

Oddly enough, Paula found that this thought did not
upset her. It was curiosity, not jealousy, that was her pre-
dominant emotion when the name of Veronica came up.
Josephine had spoken as if Veronica was actually on the
ship, but from the conversation that Paula had overheard
yesterday it sounded as if Veronica belonged to the recent
past. If she and Louis ever did succeed in exchanging confidences again, thought Paula, this must be an early topic
of conversation.

"What was the other thing?" asked the nurse with ill-
disguised impatience. "You said there were two things you
wanted to say before leaving me with my patient?"

"Oh yes. It's about the injections. Mrs. Hillman seems
to have some sort of phobia of them. She told me several
times that she didn't want an injection, and I promised to
let you know when you arrived."

"Thank you," said the nurse. "I've noted it."

And she stood there, balancing herself with ease against
the motion of the ship and expecting Paula to go. She was
a handsome young woman, with well-shaped features, but
there was no warmth in the pale blue eyes. Competent and
cold, thought Paula; I would not like her to nurse me if I
were ill. She felt a qualm for Josephine's sake, but could
think of no reason to remain in the cabin any longer.

But at least she could lie on her bed and put an ear to
the partition and listen, and indeed she was not sorry to

lie down for a little, after all the strain and tension next door, and the constant struggle with the rolling motion of the ship.

At first there was nothing to be heard except the Canadian voice calling urgently: "Mrs. Hillman—are you all right? Shall I come in?"

She's at the bathroom door, thought Paula, and Josephine is still very much otherwise occupied, poor thing.

"Mrs. Hillman!" The voice was a shade higher. "Are you all right?"

After that Paula heard some unidentifiable sounds, and then a sort of stifled scream and then a clang of metal, as if one of the ship's heavy doors had swung shut. Then a short silence, during which Paula lay anxiously wondering what had happened. That scream must have come from Josephine. It seemed to link up with the stifled sobbing on the first night of the voyage that had drawn Paula into the affairs of Cabin 3033, though it could, she supposed, just possibly have been the nurse, shocked for a moment out of her professional detachment. But if so, why?

The next sound Paula heard was the nurse's voice, almost shrill now, and quite alarmed. No, not so much alarmed: it was angry.

"Mrs. Hillman!" There came a tapping sound. "Will you open this door please! At once. You must never lock yourself in when you are ill. Open this door immediately."

So that was what had happened. The events of the last few minutes settled into place in Paula's mind. Josephine must have opened the bathroom door, but only a little way; seen the nurse, given her scream, and then instantly slammed the door in the nurse's face and locked it again. Did the door lock from inside?

Paula got up to investigate her own shower room. The door was similar to that of the cabin door, with a keyhole on the outside, and a knob inside which you could turn to

lock and unlock. She took out her cabin key. It fitted the
lock. So that anybody who had the key of Cabin 3033 or
a steward's master key would be able to get in. Presumably
the nurse had no master key, but she might be hoping to
find Josephine's key somewhere in the cabin. Probably she
was looking for it now. Hence the silence.

But of course she was not going to find that key, for
Paula had seen Josephine thrust it deep into the pocket of
her dressing gown, which was no flimsy affair like the
evening dresses in the shopping arcade, but a solid, ser-
viceable, quilted gown with deep pockets. Josephine had
wanted to have that key with her, and she would certainly
not let it fall out again if she could possibly help it.

So the nurse would search in vain, and Josephine would
be safe in the bathroom until either Louis or one of the
stewards arrived. But safe from what? As Paula tried to
imagine herself in Josephine's position, she found that she
was actually breathing more rapidly, as if she had absorbed something of Josephine's hunted panic. Colin
Knight was of course enough to make anybody feel hunted,
whether or not one was closely related to him, but Paula
had gained the impression that in spite of his crude behaviour, there was in him some little nugget of affection
for his mother. In any case, since she was financially supporting him and would probably continue to do so in spite
of her threats, it would hardly be in his interests for her
to come to harm.

But it would be in Louis' interests, professionally, emo-
tionally, in every way except perhaps financially. Perhaps
even that too, since he was next of kin and must inherit
unless Josephine had left her money to somebody else.
This must worry Colin.

So Josephine might have cause to be afraid of Louis,
thought Paula, now standing at her cabin door, and perhaps of Colin too. But neither of them was there now: it

was against the nurse that Josephine had locked herself in. Was her horror of injections as bad as all that?

Suddenly she was overwhelmed by the sense of Josephine's helplessness and fear and by her own inability to be of any use. Her vague apprehensions had turned into an almost unbearable sense of impending tragedy. She tried to tell herself that it was largely due to the storm: all the passengers on the ship, however brave a face they put on it, must be feeling ill at ease even if not physically ill, but she knew in her heart that it was not only the near-hurricane conditions. She had stumbled into, or had deliberately walked into, a human situation that had reached its crisis and she was haunted by the feeling that it was going to end in disaster.

What I need, thought Paula, is a good dose of Mercy Fordham, and she picked up the telephone and dialled Mercy's cabin number. Nobody replied, and after a couple of rings she hastily rang off, remembering that Eugene was ill in bed and ought not to be disturbed.

Perhaps Mercy was in the lounge. Paula had a great urge to be doing something definite, rather than just staying down here and listening and worrying. She made her way along to the port side corridor on Three Deck and paused for a moment, wondering which staircase or elevator to use.

A man came hurrying towards her from the front end of the ship, balancing himself by stretching out both arms and pushing at first one side of the corridor and then the other. He was as practised as any professional sailor, and her first thought was of Louis, but the man was not tall enough. He came nearer and she saw the dark beard and pug-like features of Colin Knight, and for the first time since they had met she actually felt quite glad to see him.

"Is Louis there?" he asked.

The aggressiveness and sarcasm were gone; he looked and sounded just a worried young man.

"I don't think so," replied Paula. "But the nurse is still there. And Colin—"

He was edging past her to get to Cabin 3033. She caught his arm.

"Colin—it sounds as if your mother has locked herself into the bathroom and the nurse is trying to persuade her to come out. I know she's frightened of injections, but after all, with a trained nurse—"

"Nurse!" cried Colin. "She's a phoney."

Paula's heart seemed to give a lurch in rhythm with the ship. The sense of impending disaster went into a crescendo.

"Oh, she's well qualified and has been on this ship for the last three months," went on Colin. "I've just been down to the hospital to check. What they hadn't known—and it doesn't matter to them of course—was something I realized as soon as they gave me her name. She happens to be a distant cousin of Louis, and it's my belief that there's a lot more between them than cousinship. Her name is Veronica Lander."

Paula's heart seemed to lurch in the opposite direction. No wonder Josephine had screamed when she opened the bathroom door; no wonder she had slammed it again and locked herself in.

"I see my mother has been talking to you," said Colin, "and I propose now to have a little talk with Nurse Lander."

"Isn't there anything at all I can do?" asked Paula.

"Thanks, but I think you'd better leave this to me. Unless you'd like to leave your cabin door open. I might be glad to use the phone."

He left her abruptly and went into Cabin 3033. Paula returned to her own cabin and sat down on the bed.

Veronica. Well at least that answered one big question and also made more sense of Josephine's fear. But it opened up a whole new area of doubt and suspicion. Could there be a deep-laid plot between Louis and Veronica? Colin was certainly acting as if he thought so, but then Paula did not trust Colin either, and if there had to be a villain she would rather it were Colin than Louis. The thought of Louis being so two-faced was very disagreeable indeed, but there was no doubt that he was a good actor. A man who had turned himself from a homeless refugee boy into a well-established English novelist must be gifted in playing a part.

Paula could hear the voices of Colin and Nurse Lander from the other side of the partition. They were talking more quietly than she would have expected in the circumstances, and she could not hear what was being said. She hoped that Colin would insist on his mother's being taken to hospital, because that seemed the only way in which she could be looked after in peace and safety, but perhaps Josephine would refuse to go, knowing that Veronica was working there.

Poor Josephine. She did indeed seem to be in a trap. Paula cast around in her mind for some positive way in which she could help her. There was no point trying to intervene anymore herself, but perhaps another nurse, or a doctor, or even a stewardess . . .

Jenny seemed to be a competent and sensible person. Surely she could be persuaded to go in and use her master key to release Josephine, who was not so sick that she could not stand up for herself against Nurse Lander, with Jenny and Colin there to support her.

Paula pressed the bell. To her surprise the knock came at the door almost immediately. Jenny must have been just outside.

"Come in!" she called, and then, a second later: "Denis! I thought you were off duty and asleep."

He smiled a trifle sheepishly.

"I don't really sleep till afternoon. It's just a manner of speaking. I have some breakfast and a visit to the pub—

we've got a pub, you know, darts board and all. And—
er—what you might call a bit of social life—''

A good old gossip, thought Paula.

"But with the storm, and some of the new lads feeling
a bit rough, I told Jenny I'd stay and help her for an hour
or two. So what can I do for you now, ma'am," he concluded, suddenly putting on his official manner.

"It's not for me," said Paula. "It's for next door."
After a moment's thought she decided to take him partially
into her confidence. "Mrs. Hillman is rather ill and she's
terrified of injections, and she begged me not to let them
give her one, but the nurse is in there now, and as far as
I know Mrs. Hillman has shut herself in the bathroom and
is afraid to come out. And there's a man who sits at our
table and seems closely connected with them all in there
too. And I feel very sorry for Mrs. Hillman and was wondering whether you or any other of the crew could help.
Couldn't we get one of the doctors along?''

Denis had been listening to her avidly. "Where is Mr.
Hillman?'' he asked when she had concluded, his wide
eyes staring straight at her with an air of great innocence.

"He went to the hospital to fetch a nurse," said Paula,
"but that was some time ago and I don't know where he
is now. Good God!'' she exclaimed. "I'd quite forgotten.
I was supposed to meet him for coffee. It's terribly late
but he may still be waiting for me. Except that with his
wife so ill one would have expected him to be down here.''

Paula was becoming rather confused, finding it difficult
to distinguish between her own fears of what might be
going to happen next door; what was actually happening
now; and what she wanted to tell Denis about it.

"Oh, for heaven's sake, can't you make some excuse to
go in and see if Mrs. Hillman is all right!'' she cried.
"I'm sure that poor woman is not being treated properly
and I daren't interfere anymore myself.''

"Okay, ma'am," said Denis, reacting much more

quickly to this direct appeal than to her careful prevari-
cations. ''I'll have a look-see.''

And he, too, disappeared into Cabin 3033, leaving Paula
feeling weary of worrying, and thinking how wonderful it
would be to go upstairs and become part of the normal
life of the ship again.

But before leaving her cabin she spared a moment to
look round and decide whether to leave it open as Colin
had requested. She did not even like the thought of his
using her phone, but it would be far more dreadful to think
that Josephine might suffer because it was not available,
and in any case she had nothing that was worth stealing
and no secrets to hide. The only thing of value was the fat
notebook in which she had recorded her items for the book
on the Goff family. She placed this in her shoulder bag
along with other essential documents and, after a moment's thought, put the two photographs in as well. It made
rather a heavy load to lug around but at least she knew
exactly what she would hold on to if ever the ship's emergency bells did ring for real.

The elevator was a long time in coming, and feeling too
restless to wait, Paula once again made her way up four
flights of stairs, clinging to the rail all the way. She felt
obliged to go and find out if Louis was still waiting for
her in the card room, though she could not help hoping
that he would not be there. The events of the last hour had
changed her feelings towards him so drastically that she
would scarcely know how to behave. How on earth could
they drink coffee and discuss the finer points of great English prose writers when all the time she was wondering
whether he had arranged with Veronica to give Josephine
an injection that would send her into a deep sleep, which
would give him the chance to—

To do what? Dispose of the body? Had not Paula herself
pointed out that this was by no means a simple undertak-
ing?

There were only three people in the card room: an old man working out chess problems by himself, and two teenage girls playing Scrabble. One of them looked up from the board as Paula came in.

"Are you Dr. Glenning?"

"Yes," said Paula.

"Then we've got a message for you," said the girl, and handed over a folded sheet of paper.

The Scrabble game did not appear to be very absorbing, because they stopped playing and watched Paula as she read.

"Eleven-thirty," was written at the top. "I'm sorry I can't wait any longer. I must go and see how Josephine is. Same place after dinner again if all well?"

The handwriting was large and sloping, with extravagant capital letters and long loops to the "y" and the "g."

"He seemed very disappointed," ventured the girl who had handed Paula the paper.

"But glad when we came in so that there was somebody he could leave a message with," said the other, "since there'd been nobody else here. Only the old guy in the corner, who wouldn't notice if the ship caught fire."

"He was rather nice." The first girl spoke again. "Quaint, but good-looking and with very good manners. We quite fancied him."

The two young faces looked hopefully at Paula. They must be about twelve and thirteen, she thought, and speaking with a Lancashire accent. Probably sisters. And probably belonging to the hoi polloi of the passengers, the cut-price tour of five American cities. They did not look like seasoned travellers, but like children who did not know what to do with themselves and were ready to find amusement wherever it could be had.

"He's an author," said Paula. "I met him at a lecture

yesterday morning. And I teach English Literature and we wanted to continue our discussion, but I got delayed.''

The girls looked mildly interested, but it was plain that they did not think this a very promising start to a shipboard romance. Paula asked them about themselves and found that she was correct in placing them with the special offer tour. Apparently they had not enjoyed it as much as expected and would be glad to be home. And now Mum and Dad weren't feeling well and the friends of their own age whom they had been with yesterday had not appeared this morning either and they were feeling fed up and bored.

Paula mentioned the children's room on the Sports Deck, where a trained staff was said to organize entertainment and activity all day long, and was told, with some indignation, that it was nothing but a kids' nursery. She then asked if she might join them at Scrabble, and was made welcome at the table. With her larger vocabulary and greater mental liveliness the game perked up considerably, and they played until lunch-time and parted with good will on all sides, the girls asking if she would come and play with them again, and Paula feeling very grateful indeed for what had proved an ideal distraction from her own restlessness and agitation.

She was also grateful to the girls for helping her to a more balanced view of Louis, for the coming into different company had made her realize just how much she had been influenced by the hysterical atmosphere in Cabin 3033. That he would like to be free from Josephine was surely beyond all doubt, and Paula's suspicions might well have some foundation. But on the other hand, he could equally well be innocent of any evil intent, and the girls' account of their own impressions of him helped to restore Paula's own original image to her mind and brought her some ease.

10

Paula was the first to arrive at her table for lunch. There were rather more people in the dining room than there had been at breakfast, but the ship was rolling as much as ever, and there was still a tendency for crockery and cutlery and even chairs to slide about.

The Chinese steward actually smiled at her of his own accord, and she asked him whether he thought the storm would continue for much longer.

"The forecast is better," he replied. "This evening is sunshine."

"That's a relief. Although I feel I am very lucky to be on my feet. Do you ever get seasick?"

"Once," he said, holding up a forefinger. "Just once."

"I suppose one does get used to it," said Paula, and it looked as if they might be about to sustain quite a respectable conversation, but at that moment Mercy Fordham arrived, followed by Eugene, who looked pale but was as upright as ever.

Paula greeted them warmly and the steward helped them into their seats. "Monsieur is better?" he murmured.

"Thank you, yes," said Eugene. "Due to some wonder drug that they produced at the hospital." He picked up his menu and smiled at Paula. "And you stayed on your feet, you clever girl."

"Just good luck," she said, and began to study the menu.

She felt as if she had known the Fordhams for years instead of having met for the first time two days ago, and to be sitting down to lunch with them was the most normal and natural and comforting thing in the world.

"Roast pork and red cabbage!" exclaimed Mercy. "Are you crazy, Eugene Fordham? No, he will not have roast pork," she said to the steward. "He will have poached halibut and boiled potatoes and I shall do the same."

Paula, who was feeling hungry again and who had been tempted by the richer and heavier dishes, decided to follow Mercy's self-sacrificing example so that Eugene did not have to look at what he was missing. He raised an eyebrow when Paula made her choice and then nodded to show he appreciated it.

"I've got a little mite of a suspicion, but maybe it's only wishful thinking," said Mercy, "that we are going to be spared the company of Mr. Colin Knight."

Paula asked for her reasons.

"Because we ran into him—yes, literally ran into him—in the Midships Lounge a short while back, speeding away on a matter of life and death."

"Now, honey, don't exaggerate," interposed Eugene.

"Colin said so himself," protested Mercy. "He said his mother was very ill, and he'd only come up to get the latest weather forecast and find out if there was any chance of the storm abating, and he had to hurry back at once to her cabin. Next door to yours," she added, giving Paula one of her innocent-old-lady looks.

"All right," said Paula, "I'm going to tell you all about it in a minute, but first of all, could you tell me what you talked about to Colin after breakfast, when you'd got rid of me. Oh, I didn't mind," she went on hurriedly, seeing Mercy look a little ashamed and Eugene rather puzzled,

"I knew you wanted to have another go at Colin on your own. What did he say?"

"Nothing of interest. I had my due reward for being mean to you," said Mercy. "He became very maudlin over his dear old dad, and I had to hear the whole story twice over. Then he said he'd better go and take a look at his ma, and I guess you can carry on from there, Paula."

Paula did so, holding her audience enthralled, and holding back very little of what she had heard and seen. Eugene was at first inclined to think that the whole thing was hysteria on the part of Josephine, who seemed to become uncontrollably jealous if her husband showed any interest in another woman, but Mercy thought there was more to it than that.

"What I should like to know," she said, "is how much money Josephine has and who does it go to if she dies. And is she one of those people who are always changing their will? She looks to me the sort who—"

She broke off suddenly and turned to Paula, who had not realized that she had made any sound.

"I've just remembered," she said as Mercy continued to look enquiringly at her. "It's probably of no significance at all."

And she told them of the sheet of paper wound into the typewriter in Cabin 3033, with the one word "Draft" typed on it.

"That could mean anything," said Eugene. "I'm always putting sheets of paper into the typewriter and typing 'Draft' on them. There's one hell of a lot of things I want to protest about nowadays, and it makes me feel good, even if I never get any further."

"Draft," repeated Mercy thoughtfully. "It could be the draft of a new will. How's this for a scenario, folks? Josephine has had enough of supporting the two of them—her husband and her son. You heard her say so herself. And now they have both offended her way past any forgiveness—Louis with his girl friend, and Colin—well, we've all seen what Colin can be like. So she's going to leave all her money to—''

"You need witnesses to a will," put in Eugene mildly, "and they must not be personally involved. How is Josephine going to draft a will and have it signed and witnessed without either her husband or her son knowing about it?''

They all thought this over for a moment or two and then Mercy said: "Her husband would have to know. Yes, I guess that's how it was. Mr. Hillman has persuaded her to make a new will leaving everything to him and nothing to Colin, and Colin gets to hear of it. Thus his sudden concern for his mother.''

"Colin is capable of anything," said Paula, "but I wouldn't have thought Louis was particularly mercenary.''

The Fordhams exchanged glances. Mercy said: "I don't see any reason why he shouldn't be. I'm sorry, Paula.''

"Oh, you don't need to worry about me," cried Paula. "I'm not falling in love with him, I promise you. But I think that maybe I have a little fallen in love with my idea of him as a stifled genius. That stuff he quoted last night was good. Honestly, Mercy, it was good. In quite a different category from his published books.''

"Paula, I don't doubt it. You're a very good judge. But what I just can't credit is that somebody who has got talent—real talent—can go on all these years without using it. Okay, so you're going to tell me he's written this book that's so good and he daren't publish it because his wife would not approve. No." Mercy shook her head vigorously. "I don't believe it. I just don't believe it.''

"Neither do I," said Eugene. "What was to stop him publishing it under another name? Sure she would have found out in the end and it could have led to a mighty quarrel with Josephine, but is he such a poor fish that he can't stand to quarrel with his wife? Talking of poor fish, honey, and talking of quarrelling with your wife, if you ever order poached halibut for me again—''

He broke off and looked hopefully at Paula.

''I'm not enjoying mine very much either,'' she admitted.

Mercy began to laugh. ''Okay. It's all my fault. Let's start again.''

''I'll have the chicken. That's a fair compromise,'' said Eugene. ''Now what I was saying, Paula,'' he went on presently, ''is that you can't have it both ways. Either this guy is some sort of minor genius, in which case he has to bust out with it in some way or other, and he isn't going to wait for twenty years before breaking the story of his magnum opus to a stranger on an ocean liner, even if she does happen to be a charming young teacher of English Literature. Or else he isn't a genius at all, but he just wants to make an impression on the young lady, playing the tragic role of one of the great might-have-beens if it hadn't been for the selfish and cruel woman he married.''

''But he does argue about it with his wife,'' protested Paula. ''I heard them.''

''So he plays the frustrated genius role with her as well. It must have driven her crazy. What I don't understand,'' went on Eugene, cutting up his chicken with relish before taking up his fork to eat, ''is why she puts up with him.''

''Because she loves him,'' said Paula, rather taken aback by this unexpected onslaught from Eugene, for she had assumed that it was Mercy who was the formidable one of this partnership. Perhaps Mercy was trying to spare her. ''The sort of woman whom other women's husbands believe they could be happy with.'' It all fitted in. It was painful to have her original idea of Louis knocked about in this way, but all the same, she told herself, whatever he really was, potential murderer or pathetic phoney or both, one thing was certain: he had helped her to come to and sustain a difficult decision, helped her onto the right but difficult path, and nothing could take that away.

As for Mercy and Eugene, she had been longing for a great draught of their robust common sense, and she ought not to complain when she got it.

"I suppose he could enjoy playing the stifled genius and misunderstood husband with younger women," she said, thinking that this must be the case with Veronica and no doubt others as well, "but I still keep coming back to that stuff of his he quoted. It was good."

"It was good," said Mercy quietly. "Okay. We believe you. But can you be sure that it was his own?"

"Good Lord." This was a new thought for Paula. "It never occurred to me to doubt it. It fitted in so naturally with what we'd been talking about. It seemed to come naturally out of his own life and personality."

"It might be," said Mercy, "that he's one of those writers who produce just one good story or one good line of verse. I've always thought that must be even worse than not being able to produce anything worthwhile at all."

"Could be," said Eugene, "or it could be that he was quoting something he'd read that slotted in with his own experience. Did it remind you of any author you know?"

Paula thought this over. "No," she said at last. "It just never occurred to me that it was not his own."

"There seems to be some sort of role reversal here at this table," said Eugene. "It's we Americans who are said to be the simple and credulous ones, and you Europeans who are full of subtleties and suspicion."

"You're way out of date, Gene," said his wife. "That's the Henry James theme."

"And it's still true for the most part," declared Eugene, "but maybe not right at this moment. I don't know how it is in British universities, Paula, but in our schools we are plagued with plagiarism."

"Plagiarism?" echoed Paula.

"Sure. Students passing off large chunks of quotation as if it were their own original work. Our son and his wife are both college teachers and they complain about it all the time. Don't your students do it?"

"Not that I know of," said Paula, frowning. "Every now and then somebody paraphrases a section of a book. I once set an essay on James Joyce which was obviously more than the class could cope with, and several of them came up with the same set of statements which they could hardly have thought of for themselves and which were obviously taken from a critical essay that was at the head of their reading list, but I honestly can't remember a case of anybody actually copying from a text. I wonder that they can expect to get away with it."

"They are quite clever," said Eugene. "They wouldn't copy out some well-known piece of criticism that the teacher would instantly recognize, but they select lesser-known passages from well-known authors and critics and don't even bother to paraphrase them."

Paula was interested, and would have continued the discussion longer, but the notion that Louis might have been quoting from somebody else's writing was eating away at her mind and she could not help reverting to it.

"It's a pity," said Eugene, "that you haven't got a sample of his handwriting. Mercy worked as a graphologist some time back. She might have been able to give us a few clues."

"But I have got a sample," cried Paula, and began to rummage in her shoulder bag. "Yes, here it is. I nearly threw it away."

Mercy studied the little slip of paper that the girls in the card room had handed to Paula, while Eugene ate his ice cream and Paula, feeling vaguely guilty as if she had committed some sort of treason against Louis, stared across the dining table to the windows at the far side.

From where she sat, she could see only the sky. Even

when the *Gloriana* dipped right over in that direction, the horizon did not become visible. But there seemed to be some signs of a break in the grey, a thinning of the cloud rather than an actual gleam of sunlight.

"This is very interesting," said Mercy. "It's too small a sample to do any kind of thorough analysis, but there are one or two features that are quite marked. The decorated capital letters, the size of the long letters. There looks to be a lot of fantasy here. Day-dreaming. *Folie de grandeur.* It could be comparatively harmless or it could be the sort of illusion that leads to lying and pretence. A complex character. Not stable. Not at peace." She looked up at Paula. "But that does not exclude a genuine creative gift. After all, the art of fiction is the art of illusion."

"So what's your opinion, honey?" asked Eugene. "Would this guy quote somebody else's work as his own in order to impress a young lady?"

"Oh yes," replied Mercy. "That looks very possible. But it's only my opinion," she added, "and if I had a better sample I might well find some balancing features."

There was a short silence. Then at last Paula stopped staring at the sky, in which there was now appearing a faint glimmer of light, and looked straight at Mercy.

"I think you may well be right," she said. "I think Louis Hillman has done that act before, and probably needs to do it in order to keep up his self-image. I don't believe there is a manuscript of his locked away in a drawer in their Sussex home. Or if there is one, then it's not much good. And I think Josephine knows it all. And he knows she knows, but still has to play out his role. And that scene I overheard must have been enacted many times before."

"I guess you're right," murmured Mercy. "I guess they both of them know the score."

"But Veronica may not know the score," went on Paula. "Veronica may genuinely believe in freeing Louis' genius from the stranglehold of his wife."

"Maybe," put in Eugene, "or maybe she just believes in getting hold of Josephine's money."

"But if the business is really going downhill," began Paula.

"You've only Colin's word for that. Personally I'd say Josephine has money, and that she's got the sense not to let either Louis or Colin know how much."

It sounded very plausible reasoning to Paula. It also sounded rather depressing. Something in her was still clinging to the idea of the writer trying to release his true gifts, and to have the whole situation reduced to a matter of people scheming to inherit money was too painful an anticlimax. The only advantage to be gained from the Fordhams' view of the whole affair was that it did make Louis rather less likely to be a murderer.

But Josephine's fear had been very real. Horribly real. That was something Paula had seen and heard for herself and she was not going to give it up for all Mercy's reasoning and Eugene's worldly wisdom.

"I'm going down to see what's been happening," she said. "And also to lock my cabin door. I don't trust Colin at all, but he won't have found anything. Not even a string of fake pearls."

Mercy stretched out a hand to detain her. "Do take care, Paula. We'd hate you to come to any harm."

She spoke very seriously. Paula smiled down on the worried upturned face. "I'm all right. Truly. There's no need to worry about me. I just feel rather sad at the idea of Louis Hillman being a fake. Just like his novels. But I'm sure you're right about it."

"I wasn't talking about your feelings," said Mercy. "I'm thinking of your personal safety."

"My safety?" Paula was surprised. "I don't see how I can be in any danger. Unless the storm gets worse again and the ship goes down. In which case we are all of us in the same boat. Literally."

"I haven't the least doubt," rejoined Mercy, "that this ship is going to arrive safely at Southampton next Saturday afternoon. But I do believe you have gotten yourself involved in a very tense and potentially a very disagreeable situation and I wish you would ask to change your cabin."

The last words came out in a rush. Eugene looked almost as surprised as Paula.

"It's not like you, honey," he began, "to be so—"

"Sorry, folks." Mercy interrupted him as she got to her feet. "I'm not feeling too good. Maybe I ought not to have eaten that banana trifle. Excuse me."

And she hurried away, grasping at one chair back after another until she was out of the room. Paula expected Eugene to follow her, but he did not get up from the table. He was shaking his head. "I don't believe it," he said slowly.

"You don't believe I have any cause to be alarmed for myself?"

"That's something I don't know. No. I don't believe she's feeling nauseous."

"Then what's the matter with her, Eugene?"

"She's worried, that's for sure."

Paula thought he was going to say something else, but he didn't.

"Do you really believe in the analysis of handwriting?" she asked. "I mean the very detailed and exact analysis, not just a sort of vague general impression of the sort of person who would write like that."

"Nobody is infallible," he replied. "Graphologists can make as many errors as anybody else. But Mercy is very seldom wrong."

"What you are saying," said Paula slowly, "is that you think she has read something in Louis Hillman's writing that has alarmed her and that she doesn't want to tell me?"

"I guess that's just about it," said Eugene.

11

So Mercy does now think that Louis is capable of murder, said Paula to herself as she made her way out of the dining room. She was not taking it very seriously before, but now she has read that writing, she is.

Just outside the doors to the dining room there was a fire hydrant fixed to the outer wall of the ship. Paula took hold of this to steady herself while she paused to look out to sea. It was getting lighter every minute and there was blue sky to be seen. Perhaps it might be possible after all to go up onto the Boat Deck and breathe a little fresh air today.

But she would go alone. Not with Louis. It would be too embarrassing, now that Paula was so doubtful of his sincerity. Yet she could not feel ashamed for having been taken in, for he had seemed so very genuine at the time, and now that she was away from the immediate pressure of the Fordhams' scepticism, some obstinate little part of herself was beginning to suggest that Louis was indeed just what he seemed to be.

People, coming out of the dining room, noticed her holding onto the bright red cylinder of the fire hydrant, and asked if she was ill and in need of help. This was not the best place to stand in reverie.

"No thanks," answered Paula to several of these enquiries. "I'm fine."

At last, to get away from them, she walked through the
big lounge towards the staircase at the far end, oppressed
again by the sense of people, people, everywhere, and
never a spot to think. And her cabin was no longer a refuge. Perhaps Mercy was right and she ought to try to
change to another one where she knew nothing of her
neighbours and could rest in peace.

To avoid being enclosed with other people, even for a
few seconds, Paula passed by the elevators and the little
waiting group, and moved to the broad staircase, with its
golden carpet, and the brilliant tapestries on the walls.
They had become so familiar now that she barely noticed
them. The rolling of the ship had become familiar too: she
was learning to balance herself very well against it, and
could even foresee that it would feel quite strange when it
stopped.

On the lower decks the staircase split into two separate
flights of stairs, one on the starboard, and one on the port
side of the ship. Paula moved automatically towards the
latter, where her cabin was situated. On each deck, at the
foot of the stairs, was a broad landing giving access to
the two main corridors, and from this landing, on Three
Deck, it was only a short distance to Cabins 3032 and 3033.

The steps down to Three Deck were golden carpeted
like all the rest, but the walls here were undecorated. As
Paula came to the half-landing at the turn of the stairs she
saw below her, in the wide area at the bottom, a sight that
caused her to stop still and remain where she stood, holding onto the rail and staring down.

It was a high trolley, a hospital trolley, and pushing it
was a young white-coated man whom Paula had never seen
before. Near him, and helping him to guide the trolley,
was a woman in nurse's uniform whom Paula instantly
recognized as Veronica Lander. On the other side of the

trolley, the furthest from where Paula was standing on the stairs above, was Louis.

Paula instinctively drew back so that she was almost out of sight round the turn of the stairs, but none of the three looked up in her direction. All seemed to be intently occupied with guiding and controlling the trolley and leaning over it. As the little procession moved slowly from the port side to the starboard, stopping completely for a moment to avoid having to push uphill against the tilt of the ship, Paula saw who it was lying under the white cover.

The short black hair stood out against the pillow, and the face had scarcely more colour in it than the bedclothes. The eyes were closed. Louis was holding Josephine's hand and seemed to be speaking to her, though Paula could not hear what was said. But when they came to the foot of the stairs, Paula heard the nurse speak.

"It's not much longer now. Just a little way along the corridor and then down in the elevator. You'll soon be in bed in hospital where we can look after you properly."

Josephine made no response, and both Louis and the nurse straightened up to help the white-coated man manoeuvre the trolley round the awkward corner into the starboard corridor. This took some time. Paula watched until they were all out of sight.

"What was that?" asked a young and rather frightened voice close beside her.

Paula turned to see one of the girls with whom she had been playing Scrabble in the card room.

"It looks like the woman in the next cabin to mine," she replied. "She's been very seasick all this morning and all last night and they're taking her along to the ship's hospital so that they can look after her better."

"Oh, I see." The girl sounded relieved. "She looks— she looks so awful I thought she might be dead. People do die on cruises sometimes. My cousin told us. He's a policeman. He worked on cruise ships before he joined the force and he said they had so many deaths once that they had to hang up the corpses in the cold storage. Like in a butcher's shop. Sue and I thought he was making it up, and we laughed, but he swore it was perfectly true, and when I saw them down there just now—''

She broke off, looking frightened again.

''The lady is certainly not dead,'' said Paula firmly. ''She's feeling very ill and is not fit to walk to the hospital.''

''Can you die of seasickness?'' asked the girl.

''No,'' said Paula even more firmly. ''Nobody has ever died of seasickness, however bad they feel. It isn't an illness. It stops as soon as the sea calms down or you go ashore.''

''That's all right then,'' said the girl, whose name was Linda. ''The people my cousin Tom were talking about had died of heart attacks. They were very old. Cruises are always full of very old people. I don't want to go on anymore. I'd rather go pony-trekking. When are we going to play Scrabble again?''

''At tea-time, if you like,'' said Paula.

They walked slowly down the last flight of stairs together, one behind the other, holding onto the rail. At the bottom Linda stood still.

''Do you think they've got to the hospital by now?'' she asked.

It was obvious that she did not want to encounter that trolley again, and Paula could not blame her. The sight was upsetting enough even if one did not recognize the people concerned or know anything about the background events.

''I'll go and see, shall I?'' suggested Paula, and without waiting for an answer, she ran into the corridor on the starboard side of the ship. The trolley must have been taken into the service lift down to the hospital deck, for there was nobody in sight except a steward standing at the door of a cabin with a tray in his hands.

"All clear, Linda," said Paula. "See you in the card room later."

"Thanks," said the girl, and raced along the corridor, balancing herself, as Colin Knight had done, by stretching her arms out to the full and pushing against first one wall and then the other.

Paula stood looking after her. Poor child. There really had been something peculiarly shocking in the sight of that hospital trolley, with the white-clad figures beside it, and the dead white face on the pillow. It was so horribly out of place on this luxury ship, where everything was set up for leisure and comfort and amusement. It was as if the smiling mask had been stripped from the face of the clown; as if the curtain had gone up before the players were ready to put on the show, revealing all their human weaknesses, their human mortality.

But Josephine was not dead. Paula watched Linda disappear into a cabin a long way down the starboard corridor before she returned to the other side of the ship and walked the few yards to her own cabin. Josephine was not dead, but had presumably been given the antiseasickness injection in spite of all her protests and was very deeply asleep. And somebody—either Louis or Colin, or perhaps the nurse, had insisted that she should be taken to hospital, where surely she would be safer than in the cabin, even with Nurse Lander on the staff.

Surely she would be safe in the hospital. If you were afraid that somebody wished you ill, or if you were actually feeling very ill, even if only temporarily, then the best place for you was a hospital. The *Gloriana* boasted a modern, fully equipped hospital, complete with operating theatre and every conceivable variety of life-saving apparatus.

Paula recalled a fragment of conversation that she had overheard on that first confused and jostling evening meal on board the ship. An elderly American couple—there were many such on board—and the man had presumably suffered several heart attacks and the wife was reassuring him. "It's the safest place in the whole world to have a heart attack . . . no waiting or worrying about getting to the hospital . . . in four minutes they've got the whole team assembled to pull you through . . ."

And Josephine actually had a heart condition. She is best in hospital, Paula told herself firmly. It's not like some sinister little private nursing home. It's like a public hospital. You can't hide things on a ship, even a ship of this size.

She reached her cabin and stood for a moment in the passage. The door of Number 3033 was shut. It looked as blank and secret and unknown as all the other doors that she had passed as she made her way along the corridor. Just a door, a white-painted door. Like a curtain or a mask on the face, concealing all that lay behind.

Paula took out her key and fitted it into the lock of her own cabin. It would not turn, and she had a moment of puzzlement and even of fear before she remembered that the door had been left unlocked. It was not like her to get into such a state of nerves. Mercy's suggestion that she should ask for another cabin came into her mind, and was instantly suppressed. She had to find out exactly what had been going on next door; whatever had happened, she had to see it through to the end. Curiosity was stronger than any fear.

But nevertheless she received a shock when she entered her cabin. The centre light was on, and as she came in she saw in the big mirror her own reflection, with alongside it the reflection of the lily picture, and beneath that the face of Colin Knight. He was sitting in the green armchair, and he looked for a moment as startled as she looked herself. Mirrors, thought Paula; there's something very scary about mirrors when fear is in the air.

"You gave me quite a fright. Do please make yourself at home."

She spoke as sarcastically as she could; to get back to their bickering would dispel the sense of nightmare.

Colin stood up, dropping onto the floor the copy of *The New Yorker* that he had been holding.

"I thought you were never coming," he said resentfully, as if Paula had been very late for an appointment.

"Presumably you have something you wish to tell me," she said. "I'd be grateful if you would do it quickly because I'm rather tired and want to rest."

Somewhat to her disappointment he did not respond in kind, but simply said: "Mother's been taken to the hospital. Louis thought you would like to know, so I offered to wait here and tell you. He went with her, of course."

"I know," said Paula.

This did produce some effect. Colin looked alarmed again. "You know? How can you know?"

"Because I saw them. A few minutes ago as I was coming downstairs. So you can't have been waiting for me for very long."

But Colin was not to be provoked into an argument. "Did you speak to anybody?" he asked.

"No. They didn't see me. I was on the stairs and they were having hard work getting the trolley round the corner to the other side of the ship."

This seemed to reassure him. "If I were you," he said confidentially, "I'd keep out of Louis' way. The fact is that Mother is really quite ill—not just seasick. She had a fall when she was in the bathroom and hit her head on the side of the bath."

"Has she got concussion?" asked Paula, sitting down on the edge of her bed.

This was a fresh shock, and yet not entirely unexpected. Had she not herself been thinking how easy it would be to fall and hurt oneself in the shower or in the bath with the ship tipping about like this? And in any case, nothing that happened in Cabin 3033 could now come as a complete surprise.

"Yes," said Colin, seating himself again. "They say she'll be all right, but she needs full nursing care, and she's not to have any visitors."

"Not even Louis?"

Colin did not have a direct answer. "That's what's bugging him. You see, he thinks he was responsible for the accident."

"How could he be responsible?" asked Paula sharply. "Josephine had locked herself in."

"But he had the key," said Colin slowly, glancing at Paula and then looking down at his feet. "It unlocks the bathroom as well as the cabin."

"I know. Mine does too. I suppose they all do."

There was a short silence. He's trying to decide what lie to tell me, thought Paula: he's very good at being provocative and making mean and suggestive remarks, but he's not very good at straight lying. She was determined not to help him by asking outright what had actually happened. It looked to her as if he was very anxious to get his version of the story in first; otherwise why should he have been waiting in her cabin and why should he have looked so worried when she said she had already seen the hospital procession, and reassured when she said she had spoken to nobody? And it also looked as if his version of the story was going to put the blame for Josephine's accident fully on her husband.

Paula waited silently. She would not show any further signs of disbelief: she would just listen.

"After you left," said Colin presently, "I tried to persuade Veronica—Nurse Lander I suppose we ought to call her—to take my mother to the hospital. And I also knocked on the bathroom door and called out to my mother that it was quite safe to open up, and that I was not going to leave her alone with Veronica.''

He paused. I am supposed to ask whether Josephine answered, thought Paula, but she still kept silent.

''After I'd been calling out for a minute or two,'' went on Colin, ''with Veronica constantly trying to interfere, my mother at last came to the bathroom door and asked me if Louis was there. I assured her that he was not, and that if she would open the door I'd take her straight along to the hospital myself and insist that they give her a bed there and look after her for the rest of the voyage. I had a feeling that she was beginning to weaken and I think she would have opened the door, but first of all the steward came in and we had a job to get rid of him, and then that damned Veronica had to start interfering again, and as soon as my mother heard her voice she cried that she was not coming out so long as that woman was in the cabin and she was not going to hospital with that woman nursing there.

''Then the telephone rang, and since Veronica made no attempt to answer it, I did so myself, but it was the hospital receptionist asking if Nurse Lander was still in Cabin 3033, because she was urgently needed for a passenger in one of the staterooms on the Boat Deck. She couldn't argue with that, and she went off looking very annoyed, and saying she'd be back shortly, but I was pleased because it gave me a chance to reassure my mother that there really was nobody in the cabin but myself. And I'm quite sure she would have come out, and we could have discussed the whole business reasonably, or as reasonably as she felt fit for, and decided what best to do, but at that moment the cabin door opened and there was Louis.''

Another pause. If this is all true, thought Paula, then Louis can't have come straight down here after giving the message for me to those girls in the card room. He must have gone somewhere else first. To the hospital again—to try to speak to Veronica on her own and find out how their plot was going? Or just to wander around the ship in the rather unhappy, purposeless sort of way that Paula had wandered around herself?

Colin was looking at her again, a sly, calculating look. I am thinking what he wants me to, said Paula to herself: that Louis and Veronica cooked up a foolproof way to dispose of Josephine, and that he, Colin, foiled their plot. Except that he has not foiled it, because Josephine did indeed have the "accident" after she had been frightened and hounded into a corner, and if only she had hit herself, or been hit, sufficiently hard, then the scheme would have been successful.

Would they try again? In the hospital? The nurses would presumably have a rota of duty hours. If Veronica was left in sole charge, would she be able to arrange that Josephine did not recover?

At this stage in her rapid reasonings Paula found it very difficult to remain silent and apparently unmoved. Forget Josephine for the moment, she told herself, and concentrate on what Colin is saying. Keep careful mental note of his story so that you can compare it with what you hear from the other people involved.

"There was Louis," repeated Colin after waiting in vain for Paula to respond. "And that put paid to all my hopes of keeping Mother calm. Before I even had a chance to warn him to speak quietly—not that he'd have taken any notice of me if I had—he began to shout at me—what was I doing there, where was the nurse—and then he called out to Josephine and of course she heard it all and made some sort of noise that showed him she was in the bathroom. I'd been going to try to tell him she'd been taken to hospital. That's when it happened."

Another pause. It's very true, thought Paula, that if you listen without interrupting and just let people talk they are very likely to say more than they wanted to, especially if they are not telling the exact truth. But the silence lasted so long this time that she felt obliged to react. Besides, Colin's story was obviously nearly at an end and it was equally obvious what that end was going to be.

"He tried the bathroom door, I suppose," she said.

"He did that," said Colin eagerly, "and rattled the handle, and called out to her and she didn't answer, and then he muttered a bit to himself and tried the key of the cabin and opened the bathroom door and went in and the ship was just at that moment heaving over—like it's doing just now—and there was an awful crash and I staggered for a second or two and then Louis came out of the bathroom and said, 'Call the hospital quick. She's fallen and hit her head on the edge of the bath.' "

12

"Your poor mother," said Paula softly. "She was feeling so sick and giddy, and then all this coming and going and shouting at her . . . your poor mother."

The sympathy was sincerely felt, but it also gave Paula a breathing space before responding to Colin's story. What he now wanted was for Paula herself to hint that Josephine's fall might not have been completely accidental, so that they could embark on a cosy little discussion of their suspicions of Louis.

It was very difficult indeed not to fall into the trap, since Paula's suspicions of Louis were in any case very strong, and Colin was very skilful at arousing the reactions he wanted. To pity Josephine was a safe move. Colin was obliged to join in, and indeed Paula still had the impression that he was not being entirely hypocritical and that he did have some sort of feeling for his mother.

Then she said slowly, feeling her way: "It must have been an awful shock for Louis, and for you too. Did you have to wait long for the doctor?"

"We didn't get a doctor immediately," replied Colin. "Nurse Lander came back just as we were lifting my mother onto the bed, and she examined her and said it was a concussion, and after that she took over, called the hospital, had a talk with one of the doctors, arranged that

116

he would get along as soon as he could, and that they would take Mother in as soon as they could get a bed ready—which turned out to be not for another hour or more. They've apparently been very busy with storm casualties—broken arms in the crew's quarters and such-like.''

"Poor things," said Paula, since she seemed to be expected to say something.

"I didn't actually see the doctor myself," went on Colin. "Nurse Lander had to go again as soon as she'd made Mother as comfortable as possible, and she told Louis what to do when Mother became conscious. I'd like to have stayed"—here was a short pause for a glance at Paula—"but I didn't exactly feel *persona grata* at the moment. I daresay you've already guessed that Louis and I are not exactly buddies. I don't consider that marrying him was the wisest thing she ever did, and he can never get over the fact that I have what you might call a prior claim on her.''

Money, thought Paula; that's what this is about. Eugene Fordham, you were right in that respect.

"I suppose there are always difficulties in this sort of relationship," she said vaguely.

"Oh yes. Mother and I have had our tiffs as well. But they aren't serious. It's been different in the case of Louis.''

Here we go again, said Paula to herself; he is determined to have us talk about the tension between Louis and Josephine, and if I don't say something soon he is going to get suspicious of me too.

She had not, up till this moment, been actively afraid of Colin, but the sudden sight of him in her cabin had given her a shock and she wished they were having this conversation in a more public place. She did not like those mean and calculating looks that he kept giving her, and she began to wonder whether he had ever actually threat-

ened Josephine. It was easy to believe that there was a
vicious streak in his character.

At this moment she would far rather have been talking
to Louis, even though she believed that Louis had the
greater motive for causing Josephine's "accident," and
even though she had seen for herself that Josephine did
not appear to be afraid of Colin. It had been the sight of
Veronica that had sent her into hiding, and between Veronica and Louis, in Josephine's opinion, there was much
more than a distant cousinship.

But I am not going to make any comment, decided
Paula, neither to Colin nor to anybody else, not even to
the Fordhams, until I've heard Louis' side of the story. And
after that I shall judge for myself.

She got up from the bed, aiming to do it in a decisive
and dismissive manner, but the effect was spoilt by another particularly heavy roll of the ship, which made her
clutch the dressing table for support. Colin remained
seated.

"Colin," she said, "I'm afraid I'll have to go now. I
really came down to fetch a book that I'd promised to give
the librarian. And of course to find out how your mother
was," she added hastily, thinking that this sounded to un-
believably casual and indifferent. "I suppose there's no
point in my going down to the hospital, but I shall telephone to find out how she is. And I'll send her some
flowers. There's a florist's shop up in the arcade."

"What a very kind and generous thought," said Colin
in his most sneering voice. "They'll cost you a bomb on
this ship. And all for a casual acquaintance."

"Okay," Paula suddenly blazed at him, "so I am only
a recent acquaintance, but all the same I've seen enough
of her life to be damned sorry for your mother, and if
there were anything at all I could do for her, then I would
do it. I hope they'll look after her properly in the hospital
and I hope she'll soon be better, and if I were her, when

this ship docks at Southampton I'd get rid of the lot of you, because I reckon you've just about hounded her to—''

Paula broke off as suddenly as she had begun. Her voice was racing ahead of her conscious thinking: it had very nearly said, ''hounded her to death,'' and Colin noticed it.

''That, of course,'' he said very quietly, ''is what this is all about. There is always the possibility that she will not recover consciousness. This is why Louis is so worried. As the last person to see her alive, you might almost say.''

Colin produced yet another of his calculating stares, and the *Gloriana* produced another sickening lurch. Paula collapsed onto the bed again and held her hands over her face.

''Please go away,'' she said. ''Any minute now I am going to vomit.''

He went at last. Paula, feeling genuinely ill, dragged herself to her feet, locked the door of the cabin behind him, and lay back on the bed. After a while the nausea and the giddiness passed, but she felt exceedingly thirsty. She pressed the bell by the side of the bed, and when the knock came at the door she called out, ''Is that you, Jenny?'' half-fearing that it could be Colin back again.

It was a relief to see the middle-aged woman in the blue overall, and Paula asked for some fruit juice. When Jenny returned with a bowl of fresh fruit as well as the juice, Paula asked whether Denis was still helping out.

''No, he's gone to bed,'' was the reply. ''The rush has eased off and a lot of people have recovered and got up. Are you feeling bad, madam? I can give you a tablet if you like.''

Paula refused. ''I'm much better now. It was the shock as much as anything. I saw them taking that poor woman next door to the hospital.''

"Oh yes, madam." Jenny's face was impassive. "Very sad. But we do get people having falls and hurting themselves when the sea's rough. There's two of the apprentice cooks with broken arms, poor boys."

"But nobody else with concussion?"

"Not that I know of, madam. That was very unlucky. It's better to lie still in bed when you're feeling as giddy as that and not to try to get to the bathroom. A wet floor can be dangerous, even on a calm sea."

"And even on land," said Paula. "As a matter of fact when I was having my shower this morning I sat down in it because I didn't feel safe standing up."

"Very wise precaution, madam."

"But in Cabin 3033 they've got a bath and I suppose she fell against the side of it and hit her head."

"I believe that's what happened, madam. A nasty accident."

"We'll have to hope the concussion isn't too serious and that she'll soon get over it," said Paula.

"Yes, madam," said the stewardess.

It was very plain that she was not disposed to gossip; not like Denis. But for Denis' account of events Paula would have to wait till the evening, and there were many hours to pass before then. One or two of them could be spent playing Scrabble with Linda and Sue, and after dinner there was a film that she rather wanted to see. She had also intended to explore some other parts of the ship. Apparently there was another big lounge which she had not yet seen, and a gym and a health club, and the lido, and the casino, and a lot more shops in addition to the ones in the arcade. There was also a chapel and a synagogue. Paula had no religious belief, but nevertheless found the thought of these vaguely comforting. Then there were the table-tennis rooms and the sports decks (weather permitting), and various lectures, and social get-togethers for different age groups.

The trouble was that compared with the drama that had been taking place in Cabin 3033, all other activity seemed dull and meaningless, and when she asked herself what she really wanted to do, the only answer she could give was that she wanted to have a long and uninterrupted talk with Louis, and not to have to wait until the Jacobean Bar after dinner, or the Boat Deck, for it to take place.

Was he a phoney? Was he a murderer? Was he one or the other, or neither? The questions nagged away at her mind. The impression she had received last night, of a very gifted but very frustrated and unhappy man, remained as strong as ever. Neither the Fordhams' well intentioned arguments, nor Colin's malicious hints, could take away that impression. She was more and more determined to judge for herself, in the light of the intervening events, whether she had been wrong.

But where was Louis now? Presumably still in the hospital, waiting at Josephine's bedside for her to regain consciousness. He could scarcely do otherwise. Paula reached for the telephone by the side of the bed, dialled the operator, and asked for the hospital. At least she could enquire after Josephine; as a neighbour and acquaintance she had every right to do that.

A woman's voice, with an English, not a Canadian accent, answered the phone, and Paula put her question.

"I'll have to ask Nurse Lander," said the voice. "Mrs. Hillman is her patient. Will you hold on?"

Paula waited, hoping that she would not have to speak to Veronica, from whom she could expect only the coolest and curtest of messages. But it was the English accent that informed her that there was no change in Mrs. Hillman's condition, and Paula felt able to ask whether Mr. Hillman was still with her.

"I don't think so," said the voice. "I believe he's talking to the Chief Medical Officer."

"If you should see him," said Paula, "I wonder if you'd

be kind enough to give him a message? I should be most
grateful. It's simply to say that Dr. Glenning called to
enquire how Mrs. Hillman was.''

The title ''Doctor'' had its effect. The voice, noticeably
warmer, promised to give the message.

Paula pushed aside the telephone, telling herself that
Louis must surely get in touch with her when he was free,
and meanwhile she must try to relax. She turned the radio
to the light music station, ate a peach, and leant back
against the wall, too restless in mind to listen to anything
at all demanding, and too tired to concentrate on a book.

In this position, the rocking of the ship became almost
soothing. Perhaps it really was less severe, and the stabilizers would be effective again. Somebody she had spoken
to on the first evening on board had said that they did not
function in storm conditions. And that was true of so many
of the ameliorating factors in life, she thought sleepily;
they only helped when the problem was not very bad and
you could probably have coped without their help, but
when the situation was at its worst, they did not help at
all. Nothing helped. You either survived or you didn't.

Was Josephine Black a survivor?

Paula lay and thought about her. For all the tough reputation she had acquired and the forceful manner that Paula
had seen for herself, it still seemed to her that there had
been something brittle and vulnerable about Josephine.
She had shown no sense of self-protection in her relationship with Colin's father, and in spite of all her threats,
Paula suspected that she had been much softer with Colin
than he deserved.

As for Louis, there seemed little doubt that this was her
weakest spot of all. Jealousy was the most destructive and
enfeebling of all emotions, and Josephine was very much
a prey to it. And now she was lying seriously ill with
concussion in the hospital of the *Gloriana*, and her ille-

gitimate son wanted Paula to believe that her husband was responsible for the accident that had brought this about.

Why? Out of spite towards Louis? Or to divert attention from himself?

But what could Colin possibly have done, except harass his mother still further? About money, no doubt; or about his position in her will. He could not have been responsible for the accident, because he had no key, and she would not open the door.

Wait a minute. To argue like that was to believe Colin's story. Colin had said that his mother never opened the door of the bathroom at all and that she was inside, alone, until Louis unlocked the door with his key. Suppose Colin was lying. Suppose, during the time when Colin was alone in the cabin, he had actually persuaded Josephine to open the door, and suppose he had then hit her on the head or knocked her over so that she fell against the bath? It need not have been premeditated; it could have been in the heat of another quarrel. And then he panicked and shut her in again, so that it would look like an accident. What about the key? It was not possible to lock the bathroom door from outside except with a key. Perhaps it had slipped out of Josephine's pocket again in the fall, and Colin had picked it up, used it, and been standing there begging Josephine to come out when Veronica returned. He would then have to dispose of the key, but that was easy enough. Glowing cigarette ends were not to be dropped overboard, but there was no rule against keys.

Of course if the key was still in Josephine's dressing gown pocket that theory would be disposed of straight away. Paula was very tempted to run down to the hospital at once to try to find out. But of course nobody there was going to tell her anything, and in any case they must have removed Josephine's dressing gown when they put her to bed, and they would not have replaced it when they put her on the trolley. It was tantalizing to think that the gown

might be at this moment hanging up in the cabin next
door, only a few feet away from her, and she had no means
of finding out whether the key was still in the pocket. She
might have been able to persuade Denis to use his master
key to go and look, but it was useless to ask Jenny.

And it might not, after all, be conclusive proof that
Colin had nothing to do with the accident, because he
might well have had an opportunity to replace the key
when he and Louis were lifting Josephine onto the bed.
There was no way to prove that Colin was lying, and there
would be no way to prove that Louis was telling the truth.
And Veronica would obviously support Louis, whatever
he said. The only thing that seemed certain was that Colin
would find it very difficult to brainwash Veronica into be-
lieving that Louis was responsible, as he had tried to do
with Paula.

It was useless to speculate and it was impossible not to.
The relentless trickle of conventional melody and obvious
harmony began to irritate rather than soothe. Paula
switched off the radio and picked up the copy of G. E.
Goff's *Last Judgement*.

Perhaps, now that she knew Josephine was as safe and
well cared for as she was ever likely to be on this ship,
she could turn her mind to her own affairs again. She
glanced at the introduction to the paperback edition,
thought for a moment or two of Richard, and then of G.
E. Goff, the novelist of genius. The chain of thought led
her back to Louis again.

Not in the class of G. E. Goff, of course, but of greater
merit than appeared in his published novels. If you had
great talent, and believed that somebody was stifling your
talent and preventing you from using it, and that there was
no other way to escape, would you kill to release yourself?
You would certainly feel very bitter; so resentful, in some
cases, that it would affect your whole life and that of others

around you, including the one who was keeping your mind in chains.

But would you kill?

Certainly not as a general rule, otherwise there would be an awful lot of people—probably mostly women— murdering their partners. It would probably have to be tied up with other deep resentments as well if it was to drive you to such extreme measures.

Were there any examples from literature of somebody murdering for such a motive? Paula began to search her memory, and was rewarded by finding she had hit on a train of thought that was sufficiently absorbing to take her mind off the question of what had actually happened in Cabin 3033. Plays, novels, short stories, poems, all passed through her rapid review. She was beginning to think that you were more likely to murder somebody because he threatened to reveal that you were *not* a genius than to murder him because he prevented you from revealing that you *were*, when the telephone rang.

So fascinated had she become by her own theories that she felt almost annoyed at the interruption as she picked up the receiver.

"Paula? It's Louis here. Are you all right? Did I disturb you?"

"No. I was hoping you'd call."

"Are you doing anything in particular? I was wondering whether we could meet now instead of this evening."

"That's just what I'd been hoping. Where do you think we should have most peace?"

"Certainly not on the Main Deck. I'm calling from one of those phone boxes at the entrance to the Atlanta Lounge. There's a Bingo session going on at one end and the cruise staff are putting up decorations for tonight's floor show at the other. If you could face the elements, I really think the Boat Deck would be the best place."

"I can face them," replied Paula, "though I hope it's not raining too hard."

"It's not raining at all. The clouds are almost gone and the sun's come out. It's still very windy, but if we get right up against the shelter it ought to be tolerable. I've just been up to try it out."

"I'll be there in ten minutes," promised Paula. "I've got to look in at the card room on the way and tell Linda and Sue that I won't be playing Scrabble till later."

"Are those the Lancashire lasses?"

"Yes. You made quite an impression on them."

How extraordinary, thought Paula as she replaced the telephone, that they could have such a friendly and easy conversation after all that had taken place in the last hours. But then Louis did seem to be a straightforward and comfortable person to deal with—a most welcome contrast to Colin.

It was going to be cold out on deck, even if the skies had cleared. Paula put on a thick coat and scarf, placed the paperback book for the librarian in her shoulder bag, and stood for a moment wondering if she had everything she needed.

The little cabin looked cosy and homelike. *The New Yorker* lay where Colin had dropped it on the floor, and in her hunt for the paperback book she had let other magazines fall beside it. The bedspread, which Jenny had left smooth and neat, was now crumpled and pushed to one side; a knife and the peelings of a peach lay on the plate on the tray, and there was some fruit juice left in the bottom of the glass tumbler.

It's like the snail with its shell, thought Paula; we carry our homemaking habits about with us, sometimes for thousands of miles. Even the arum lily painting, so cool and detached, seemed now to be an essential part of her own little space. She would have hated to come back and find that it had been removed or exchanged for something else.

Here was her temporary nest, which would welcome her back when she came down to Three Deck again. Outside it was the great world of the ship; and beyond that was the vastness of ocean and sky; and beyond that yet again it was no longer a matter of space, but of time, not a question of so many hundred or thousand miles from such and such a piece of land, but so many days away from the world of every day.

Paula found herself doing what she sometimes used to do as a child, when going away from a room or a house or a town. "Goodbye, cabin," she said aloud.

And then, again as it had sometimes been when she was a child, she was suddenly overcome by the absolute certainty that she was looking at the little cabin for the last time and that she would never see it again.

13

"Josephine is dead," said Louis. "She was dead when they took her to hospital."

"I think I must have known it all along," said Paula equally calmly.

They were once more sitting within the shelter of the screen on the Boat Deck, which was still glistening with spray, although the deck chairs, which had been folded away, were reasonably dry. No other passengers had ventured to sit down, but a small straggle of people, well wrapped up and looking very pleased with themselves as they battled with the wind, were walking round the deck.

"But why the charade?" asked Paula. "The nurse and the trolley and 'you'll soon be better, dear,' and all that."

"Apparently there is some sort of international agreement, a sort of law of the sea, that obliges you not to move a dead body around a ship in sight of passengers. I can't tell you the details of it. I was not in the right frame of mind, during my talk with the captain, to take in minor technicalities, but the essence of it is, that in order to shift a body to the ship's morgue, you have to pretend that it is a still living patient. As you say, a charade, and an extremely disagreeable one. But I can see the point of it."

"So can I," agreed Paula. "It was upsetting enough even when one believed the person to be alive. Poor little

Linda looked quite green over it, and she asked me just
now how the sick lady was. I told her that she was going
on as was expected. Was that right?''

"Yes. The hospital will fend off all enquiries by saying
that she is still not fit to be visited. We've only another
two days at sea. There will be an ambulance waiting to
meet the ship at Southampton and she'll be taken off at
once, before any passengers are allowed off. They are doing a post-mortem on board, and the inquest will be held
at our hometown in Sussex.''

"What about evidence?''

"I shall have to be there, of course, and Nurse Lander
will get leave to attend, but most of the medical evidence
will be in the form of statements.''

He spoke without any sign of emotion, but he looked
very tired and strained.

"Can't they hold an inquest straightaway?'' asked Paula
in the same matter-of-fact way. "I thought the captain of
a ship at sea had practically unlimited authority.''

"He has. He can even conduct a legal marriage cere-
mony if necessary.'' Louis smiled faintly. "But it's a kind
of reserve authority for emergencies. I doubt if it would
be used for a couple who wanted to be married on a ship
for publicity purposes, for example. Similarly with less
happy events, such as a fatal accident. It might have been
different if there had been any question of negligence on
the part of any of the ship's personnel.''

So intent had Paula been on the domestic drama in
Cabin 3033 that this aspect of the matter had not yet occurred to her.

"There wasn't any such negligence,'' she said after a
moment's thought.

"None at all,'' agreed Louis. "We went into that very
thoroughly. They don't want me suing them for damages.
If anybody is guilty of negligence it is I myself for not
staying with Josephine until the nurse came, but I'm sorry

to say that we had another argument—they have become increasingly frequent lately—and since she was not too sick to quarrel, I felt that she was not too sick to be left alone. So I wandered around the ship until it was time to meet you for coffee. Not in the best of moods, I confess. And when you didn't turn up, I wandered around again for a while before coming downstairs.''

"I'm sorry I didn't keep our appointment," said Paula rather stiffly. "I was talking to Josephine."

"Yes, Colin told me you were with her. I rather wondered why."

There was no reproach in his voice, but the comment itself was enough to make Paula feel rather embarrassed. After all, when they had met in the lounge after breakfast, he had said that he didn't think Josephine wanted visitors just yet. It struck her now that Louis might well feel that she herself had some explaining to do; he was not the only one who needed to account for himself.

"I heard her from my cabin," she said. "I told you I could hear quite clearly. It sounded as if she was in difficulties, and I went and knocked on the door and asked if I could help and she let me in. Was that being interfering, Louis? If so, I am sorry. But after our talk last night . . .''

Her voice faded away. In what relationship did they now stand? Had she any right to claim that they had each other's trust and respect, after all the suspicions she had been forming of him?

"Dear Paula," he replied, "it certainly wasn't being interfering, but it might have been rather rash. Josephine can be very formidable, even when feeling seasick. And also very jealous."

He smiled again and looked at her enquiringly.

"Yes." Paula decided to be completely truthful and to assume that he was being the same. How else could they conduct this conversation? "I think perhaps she did let me in because she wanted to warn me off you. And she did warn me off you, by telling me that you were only using me as a sort of cover-up for your affair with Veronica.''

It was Paula's turn to smile and look enquiring, but he did not respond.

''I'm assuming that there was an affair with Veronica,'' she went on, ''and of course I'm bursting with curiosity! Colin said she was a cousin of yours—is that true? And was she really trying to persuade you to change your style of writing? And did you know that she was working as a nurse on this ship? She said herself that she never saw you at the hospital, but just found a message that she should come to your cabin when she was free.''

Paula paused for breath. A couple walking round the deck, linked arm in arm, passed near their deck chairs and glanced at them with some interest before walking on. Paula realized that she must have looked very agitated during this last speech, and when Louis replied it was with that harsh edge to his voice that she had noticed once or twice before.

''Shall we take these questions in order? That is, if I can remember the order. Yes, Veronica Lander is the niece of the cousins with whom I stayed as a child when I was sent to Canada. Her appearance is somewhat deceptive. She is older than she looks; nearly forty. And yes again, we did have a sentimental interlude when I was last in Canada, which was two years ago. No, it is not true that Veronica was encouraging me to break away from my style of writing. I have never discussed my writing with her at all. And no, it is not true that I have been using you as some sort of cover-up for a liaison during the course of this voyage. Since you are in every way superior to Veronica, it would be more likely to be the other way about. Josephine's jealous fabrications seem to have gone completely out of control here. In any case I am too old to cope with such complications. Where have we got to in your catechism, Paula?''

Most of this speech was made in a patronizing, almost offensive, manner that was worthy of Colin, but Paula felt that she herself was hardly in a position to take offence, so she echoed the lighter tone of the last words when she replied.

"I can't remember the number of the question in my catechism, but I think the next point was, did you know that Veronica had a job as a nurse on this ship before you came aboard?"

"Ah yes, the vital point, on which rests the whole structure of suspicion and motive. If I were to write any more detective stories I should make great play with such a question during the course of working out the plot. But this is not a fantasy, it is my life, and I am telling you the truth although I do not expect you to believe me. No, I had not the slightest notion that Veronica was on this ship. Not until this morning. I have not been in touch with her at all since last Christmas and at that time she was working in a hospital in Vancouver. We parted amicably two years ago, after she had become deeply committed to somebody else, and have been on nothing but Christmas card terms ever since. The rest of my Canadian connections I have lost touch with completely. I didn't even call them when Josephine and I went to Montreal, although she was convinced that Veronica and I were having secret meetings all the time."

That fits in, thought Paula; when I overheard Josephine complaining to Louis about Veronica it could have been referring to the past; it did not mean that either of them knew that Veronica was on the ship.

"I think that brings us to the final question," went on Louis, "which as far as I can remember concerns Veronica's veracity rather than my own, but I think I can safely answer for her that she did indeed find a message at the reception desk asking for a nurse to go to Cabin 3033. I had myself left the message with the receptionist and been told that they were all very busy but that somebody would come along later that morning. We did not mention any names, since she had no cause to do so, and at that time I did not know that the names of any of the nurses on the *Gloriana* would mean anything to me.''

He paused a moment.

''The girl did, however, ask me if it was very urgent, or was it just a case of seasickness, and I had to admit that it was not actually an emergency. I saw the girl make a note of this.''

Louis paused again and remained silent for what seemed a long time. Paula wanted to assure him that she believed him, but felt that it would be wiser to say nothing, because in spite of her longing to restore the confidence between them, she could not feel completely sure that he was speaking the truth. He was a good actor. In some respects his whole life was an act, the role being that of an Englishman writing mildly amusing and very English detective stories.

But the real self, or rather the original self, was the young refugee on the ship going to Canada. Oh yes, thought Paula, I most certainly believe in that self and in its ability to express itself in words. And I also believe that Josephine has deliberately suppressed that real self, for reasons of her own, and that it has broken out at last.

So I do believe that much, her thoughts ran on in the long silence between them as they both stared ahead at the clear blue of the sky, and as the ship tilted, much more gently now, from side to side: I do believe that there is no link-up between Louis and Veronica, no plot between them to get rid of Josephine, but what I cannot be sure of is that he did not, as Colin kept hinting, contrive Josephine's accident.

Should they talk about it now? Would she be putting herself in danger if she tried to trick him into some admission? Was she in danger now? In any case, the bluff would not succeed, because he was much too clever and much too self-controlled.

It seemed that Louis was not going to break the silence.

"You said to me last night," said Paula, "that you longed to be free of Josephine and could see no hope of this unless she had a heart attack."

Again Louis smiled faintly. "I did say that indeed. A very incriminating remark and most unwise in the light of what has happened today. It was a statement of hope rather than of intention. I did sometimes wish Josephine dead. I wonder how I would have contrived it if I had ever fallen into the temptation?"

"You're laughing at me," said Paula reproachfully.

"Of course I am. What else am I supposed to do?"

"Prove to me that you didn't knock Josephine on the head," she said very brightly.

"I don't think I can. Colin is suggesting that I had the opportunity, I suppose, and he happens to be perfectly right. I'm afraid the post-mortem won't help either, because it is only going to confirm that she died from a blow on the side of the head, consistent with hitting it against the edge of the bath. So the Chief Medical Officer says."

"But what about her heart?"

"They don't think it had anything to do with it. But we shall have to wait and see."

He was rubbing a hand over his eyes as he spoke.

"Do you want me to go?" asked Paula. "I think you'd like to rest for a while."

"Don't go," he said, and felt for her hand just as Josephine had done. "You're a great comfort. You feel real. None of the rest of it seems real. It's no effort to me to keep up the farce of Josephine not being dead, because I can't believe it either."

Paula said nothing.

"I ought not to have told you," he went on presently.

"Nobody is supposed to know except the captain and the hospital staff and a few other crew members."

"And Colin."

"And Colin indeed. But I doubt if he will break confidence. He's very much in awe of the captain."

"He's been to see the captain?"

"Oh yes," was the reply. "We both had lengthy sessions with him."

"Was it about lunch-time?" asked Paula, suddenly struck with an idea.

"Just about. Why?"

"Because Colin was up in the Midships Lounge and he told Mercy Fordham that he'd come up to see what the weather was like in the hope of being able to go back and tell his mother it was improving. I suppose he was really on his way to see the captain."

"Very likely," said Louis. "By the way, Paula, I hope you don't think I'm telling you about Josephine's death simply because you are such a charming and delightful and also a trustworthy person. That's half the story, but the other half is that I'd rather you knew straightaway than that you should try to find out what had happened to her. Because you would have tried to find out, wouldn't you?"

"Yes," she admitted, feeling embarrassed at being scrutinized so closely. "I'm afraid I should certainly have gone snooping around. I seem to be cursed with as much insatiable curiosity as the Elephant's Child."

"Or the proverbial cat. Let us hope you do not meet with the same fate."

Was this just a little joke? Or a threat or a warning?

"Am I likely to get bumped off for my snooping?" she asked in the same lighthearted tone of voice.

"Not by me," he replied. "I can't answer for anybody else. But since nobody except myself appears to have had the opportunity to bump off Josephine . . .

"All the same," he added more seriously a moment

later, "I wish you'd be careful. It's not wise to be too
inquisitive. Especially when in a closed situation like a
ship at sea."

"Louis," said Paula impulsively, "Colin was trying hard
to make me think you could have been responsible for his
mother's death. Do you think that Colin himself—"

She broke off, regretting that she had spoken.

"I do truly think it is best not to talk about it," said
Louis slowly. "And the less you can think about it the
better it will be for you. How are we going to stop you
thinking about it? Do you play bridge? That seems to be
a most mind-absorbing drug."

"I don't play bridge," replied Paula with a little spurt
of irritation, "and I can't stop thinking about it. Can you?"

"Of course I can't," he retorted even more abruptly.
"I happen to have lost my wife. Remember?"

"I'm sorry," said Paula, but whether she was commis-
erating or apologizing she did not know herself. Neither
did she know why he was urging her to try not to think
about the manner of Josephine's death. It could be that he
was afraid of what she might find out, but it could equally
well be that he was concerned for her welfare. Mercy
Fordham, who could have no other concern than Paula's
welfare, had said much the same thing. Keep out of it:
change your cabin.

But she could not keep out of it, nor change her cabin,
not even though Louis was now next door alone. How
very convenient if they had indeed wanted to carry on a
shipboard affair. But the momentary impulse had gone,
although in some ways they seemed to be drawing closer
together. Not now, thought Paula, but later this evening,
or tomorrow, I am going to tackle him again about his
writing. That is the one subject that will stop me thinking
about the way Josephine died.

"Would you rather we didn't meet anymore?" she said
aloud.

"Paula!" He seemed genuinely appalled. "What makes you say that?"

"I can't promise not to mention Josephine. You must have realized by now that I am not particularly discreet and that I just babble on. Otherwise you wouldn't have thought it necessary to warn me against letting out the secret."

"Oh dear." He rubbed a hand over his eyes again. "We seem to have got out of gear somehow. I don't know how to explain what I meant. If you have a death like this at home, then it's a great shock to all concerned, but the shock is partly absorbed by all the normal and necessary activities that follow on sudden death. Informing friends and relatives, notices in the press, funeral arrangements, even inquest arrangements if necessary. It helps a lot to be doing a lot of telephoning and running around on such occasions."

"That's true," admitted Paula.

"But in this case the whole business has to go into cold storage until we reach port. Secrecy must be observed. The natural outlets for shock must be blocked and emotions suppressed. Two thousand people have paid a lot of money to be conveyed across the Atlantic in great comfort and a fatal accident to a passenger is not on the menu. The crew members can be trusted. They are used to suppressing worse disasters than this. Colin can be trusted not to let on that Josephine is dead, even if in nothing else. Are you going to make me regret that I told you, Paula?"

She gave her promise of course; there was nothing else that she could do. But all the same she had the sense of being manipulated, far more subtly and skilfully than by Colin, into a state of mind and a course of action that was in conflict with her own deepest instincts. What Louis had just said was perfectly true. The captain and the chief officers would say the same. Even the humbler members of

crew would say the same, and as she thought this, Paula
had a brief vision of Jenny the stewardess, courteous and
efficient and friendly, but also totally discreet.

Of course they could not have the news of Josephine's
death broadcast throughout the ship. And if rumour went
round that it might not have been an accident, the last half
of the voyage would be intolerable.

Of course Louis was right, and he had indeed taken a
risk in telling her. Of course she would keep up the pretence that Josephine was alive, even to the Fordhams, even
to Colin, although he and she both knew to the contrary.

But something in her still rebelled. If it had been the
captain who had been sitting there putting forward the
argument for silence, saying that the comfort—no, more
than the comfort, that the safety of the ship and its passengers made it essential to keep rumour to a minimum,
then she would have assented wholeheartedly, as no doubt
Colin had done. It was something in Louis' manner,
something in the very words he used, that had caused this
lingering doubt. It had been too slick. No, slick was not
the word. It had been too—too literary and dramatic, the
argument of a writer or an actor, not the argument of a
man in authority in a difficult situation.

But Louis was not in any position of authority on this
ship. And he was very much a writer; the sort of writer,
Paula was beginning to think, whose ability was bound up
with a gift for acting. He needed to create his own parts,
to read aloud his own words. That was why his quoting
from his manuscript last night had made such an impression on her: he had himself become the homesick and
homeless refugee boy. And with Josephine he had played
the part of the considerate husband and the moderately
successful English detective story writer.

And now he was being the responsible citizen. It was
perfectly correct, and it was also very convenient for him
if he had been in any way guilty.

Paula stared at the now brilliant sky and the dark of the ocean, against which the rail of the ship still moved up and down, but to a much lesser degree than earlier in the day. They had come through the storm; the ship was reverting to its gentle rocking motion, and more and more people were coming out on deck, exclaiming with pleasure at the sunshine and at their own restored sense of well-being.

"Am I allowed to ask just one more question on the subject of Josephine's death?"

Paula did not look at Louis as she spoke, but when he made no reply she turned to face him and saw that his eyes were closed and he seemed to be asleep.

It would be cruel to disturb him if he really was asleep. Her question could wait. Or perhaps she could find the answer to it by some other means. She would keep up the pretence that Josephine was still alive; thus far she would hold to her promise. But she was not going to stop trying to find out what had really happened, and there was one action she could take straightaway which would satisfy both these purposes.

She got up from her deck chair, quietly so as not to wake Louis, and made her way down to the shopping arcade. It all looked very familiar now, part of the background of her present life, and it was difficult to remember the sense of nightmare that had overcome her when she first lost her way there.

The florist's shop had a display worthy of Piccadilly or Fifth Avenue. Paula chose red roses and carnations, winced inwardly at the price, and produced her credit card. This would have to come out of her next month's salary. Satisfying one's curiosity was an expensive business. She thought of telling the assistant that they were for a friend who was ill in the ship's hospital, but decided that not only was it very unlikely to produce any useful information but it might actually cause unwelcome gossip. Let the girl in the florist's think that Paula was buying the flowers for a birthday or some other sort of anniversary.

"Where shall I send them, madam?" asked the florist's assistant.

"I'll take them myself," said Paula.

This did create some surprise. Apparently, it was unusual to take on the burden of carrying a bunch of flowers oneself, and apart from the florist, several people gave Paula a mildly curious glance as she stood in the elevator going down to Four Deck, where the hospital was situated, and where she had never been before.

━━ *14* ━━

The main door of the hospital was clamped open and Paula came into a small, brightly lit room, with padded benches along two of the walls, a couple of armchairs, a table with magazines, and a little desk that stood next to a closed door. She felt faintly surprised, and then wondered why she should have expected it to look like anything but a doctor's surgery or hospital waiting room.

An old man was sitting in one of the armchairs, listlessly turning over the pages of a yachting magazine, and on the bench sat a girl whose face was vaguely familiar. She glanced up as Paula came in, and since there was no member of the staff in the room, Paula came over to where she sat with one leg propped up on a stool, and asked if she knew where the receptionist was.

"I don't think she'll be long," replied the girl. "One of the nurses called her to go and help with something. What gorgeous flowers."

"Aren't they lovely. Haven't we met before somewhere?" went on Paula.

"Didn't we get lost together in the shopping arcade the first morning at sea," said the girl.

"Of course. That's it."

They beamed at each other like old friends.

"Did you ever find the deck sports?" asked Paula. "And what's happened to your leg?"

The girl made a face of disgust. "I found the deck sports and almost immediately managed to fall over and do something quite serious to my foot. Me! A swimming instructor! And then I was silly enough to try to ignore it and just hobble about, but it got so bad that I've had to have it X-rayed and am now waiting to be bandaged up. After which I've got to go to my cabin and rest it until tomorrow morning, at least. Probably longer."

Paula expressed sympathy. "What is the hospital like?"

"Just like any other. On a small scale. Small wards with two beds in each, and a sort of intensive care ward for serious cases. An operating theatre, X-ray department, physiotherapy—you name it. It's here."

"And the staff?"

"Very good. Particularly now they aren't as busy as they were this morning."

"I've met one of them. I think it was Nurse Lander. Tall, fair. Pale blue eyes."

"Sounds like the one I first told my story to. She's very efficient. By the way, my name's Julie."

"And I'm Paula."

They exchanged cabin numbers, and Julie warmly welcomed Paula's suggestion that she should bring her down some books from the library.

"I'm travelling on my own," she added, "after visiting relatives in the States, and I've palled up with an energetic crowd who aren't going to be very interested in an invalid."

They chatted for a little longer, and then a short dark girl came through the inner door and informed Julie that they were ready for her now.

"See you," said Paula. "Good luck."

"Did you want to see a doctor?" asked the dark girl when she returned.

"No thanks," replied Paula. "There's nothing the matter with me. I only wanted to leave some flowers for a patient. An acquaintance of mine. Mrs. Hillman. I believe Nurse Lander is looking after her."

Paula studied the girl for any sign of embarrassment or surprise, but she maintained a perfect composure as she replied.

"Yes, Mrs. Hillman is Nurse Lander's patient. I'm afraid she's not fit to see anybody, but I'll ask Nurse to take her the flowers."

Paula handed over the bouquet, saying chattily that she had never been into a ship's hospital before. "Do you like your job?" she asked.

"Very much," was the staid reply. "It's an excellent little hospital."

"I suppose you don't have much turnover of staff, then."

"About the average," said the girl. "People leave to get married."

After a few more such exchanges Paula could find nothing else to say, and the dark girl, though still courteous, obviously wanted to get rid of her and was grateful when the ringing of the telephone gave her an excuse.

With a sense of anticlimax and of having come to the end of the road, Paula turned away. There was nothing to be learnt here, and the best thing she could now do was to let it rest for a while, as she always did when she got stuck with something she was writing. To concentrate too hard was always counterproductive: to think about something quite different gave the subconscious mind a chance to recycle its information and come up with some new combination of facts.

But at least she had found a new acquaintance. Helping the injured Julie to pass the time would not only be something worthwhile in itself, but it would help to divert her own thoughts, as would playing Scrabble with Linda and

Sue. There was also the paperback book that she had
promised the librarian and not delivered, and this evening
there was the captain's reception for those passengers who
had not attended the previous evening's party.

Julie's cabin was on Four Deck. Paula located it, found
pen and an old envelope in her shoulder bag, and scribbled
a note saying she would come down after dinner with anything she could find that might interest Julie, and pushed
it under the cabin door. Then she looked at her watch,
saw that it was nearly half-past five and that she would
have to hurry to reach the library before it closed.

When she got there she found she had won the day's
quiz prize, a pen similar to Mercy's, and she felt quite
disproportionately pleased. The little triumph seemed to
give her a tug back into the normal life of the ship, away
from the shock and suspicion and stress associated with
the events in Cabin 3033.

She told the librarian about Julie's accident, and came
away with a little pile of books and magazines. In the
elevator and on the corridors and landings people were
congratulating each other on their recovery from seasickness and discussing what they were going to wear for the
captain's reception. The ship was a bright and festive little
world all its own, cocooned in the now peaceful ocean,
isolated from the cruelties that the nations of mankind
were inflicting on each other. Paula found herself being
infected by the party spirit and wished that she had gone
to the hairdresser instead of spending all that money on
the flowers. The only comfort was that the patients and
hospital staff would have the benefit of them, and that Julie
would be grateful to be visited.

But as she came to her own little corner of the great
ship, the feeling of unease, of unsolved mystery assailed
her again, and for a moment she wished she were indeed
in a different cabin. The door of No. 3033 looked as blank
and secretive as ever, but she knew now that a woman had

died there, only a few hours ago, in a violent manner, whether or not by the aid of a human agent.

Surely that fact in itself was enough to account for this feeling of unease. And the hesitation about going into her own cabin was because last time she had come in, the sight of Colin's face in the mirror had given her an unpleasant shock. There could be nobody there now because she had locked it, and in any case she ought to be grateful that she was indeed returning unharmed to her own cabin, and that her earlier flash of apprehension had proved unjustified.

Of course it was all exactly as she had left it, even down to the tray with the fruit juice and the copy of *The New Yorker* lying on the floor. Paula dumped on the bed the pile of books for Julie and hastily began to get ready for the party, all the time listening, listening, as if she expected to hear a moan or a cry for help from Josephine next door. But there was no sound, and the silence was more unnerving than the sounds of distress had been. If Louis was in there, then he must be asleep. Or perhaps he was still sleeping up on the Boat Deck. It was a pity she had no chance to ask him whether Josephine's cabin key had been found. But would it have helped? He might have replied that the key was in the dressing gown pocket. That would indicate that nobody else had been in the bathroom until he opened the door, but it would still not reveal whether Josephine had died by accident or by design. And if he had answered that the key was missing, would she have believed him?

Almost certainly not. There was no proof either one way or the other and there never would be. For Paula's own peace of mind she must control this craving for certainties and try to believe in his innocence. It might help a little if somebody else believed him innocent too, and she longed to discuss it with a less biased person than Colin, but she knew she must not do so.

* * *

"We were beginning to think we would never see you again," cried Mercy as Paula sat down to dinner some time later.

"I was at the very end of the queue to be presented to the captain," said Paula. "I think he must have shaken hands with eight hundred people before it got to my turn. It must be almost as bad as being the Queen."

"The organization was excellent," said Eugene, "although the whole procedure seems rather pointless to me."

"Of course it does," said his wife, "because you don't see the point of it, which is to keep people happy and occupied and to make them spend money. Some of those ladies had spent hours fixing their clothes and their makeup and their hair. And now they will all go and buy photos of themselves shaking hands with the captain." She shook her head. "You're a misogynist at heart, Gene Fordham. You don't know what makes women happy. Does he, Paula?"

"I'm afraid it didn't make me particularly happy," said Paula. "My hair feels a mess and I've never liked champagne and I was longing for my dinner."

They were talking themselves back into their friendly relationship, the three of them, as if they were coming together after having been separated for a long time. Colin Knight had not yet appeared.

"Well," said Mercy after they had ordered their meal, "I hear that our poor friend Josephine Black is in hospital."

"Yes," said Paula. "She fell in the bathroom during the storm this morning and hit her head and has quite bad concussion. I actually saw her when I went down after lunch. She seemed to be unconscious, and they were moving her on a trolley, just like in hospital, with a nurse and a porter. It gave me quite a shock, but I called the hospital later and they said she was going on as expected, and just before the reception I took her down some flowers.''

Paula hoped that this speech sounded convincing and not too rehearsed. She had been dreading this first encounter with Mercy since she herself had learnt of Josephine's death, and was glad it was taking place in the dining room, which had a particularly bustling air this evening, with the passengers using the occasion of the captain's party as a noisy thanksgiving for having come through the storm, and the stewards hurrying even more than usual to make up for the delay in starting dinner.

But of course Mercy had questions to ask, and Paula did her best. Yes, she had first heard the news from Colin, who seemed to be genuinely upset. And yes, she had had a talk with Louis too, up on the Boat Deck as before. He was very tired, and she had actually left him asleep up there in a deck chair and had not seen him since. No, it didn't look as if there was any chance of Josephine's leaving the hospital for the rest of the voyage, and unless there was a marked improvement she wouldn't be able to see any visitors.

Except Louis?

Well, yes. Presumably he'd be allowed to sit with her. Paula didn't know about Colin. And she had not seen Veronica when she went down to the hospital with the flowers, but only the receptionist.

The arrival of their meal provided Paula with a short relief, but Mercy returned to the enquiry as soon as she could.

''Who was there when Josephine had the fall?''

''Just Louis and Colin, I think,'' replied Paula. ''Apparently Josephine was still locked in the bathroom and refused to come out, and then the ship gave a heavy roll over, and they heard the crash and Louis opened the bathroom door with his key.''

Paula was trying hard, but she knew that she was not

talking in the completely open manner that she had used at lunch-time and that Mercy had scented that she was holding something back.

Eugene came to the rescue.

"I'm getting just a mite tired of the subject of Josephine Black, and I guess Paula is too. Shall we talk about something else?"

There followed a silence between them, during which Paula thought unhappily that this must be the end of her pleasant acquaintanceship with the Fordhams, because there was no way that she could fend off Mercy's curiosity without becoming so secretive that she would give offence. It then occurred to her that this was rather how Louis must have felt when confronted with her own inquisitiveness, and she felt quite ashamed. It seemed that there was something about life on this ship, this isolated floating city, that led people to shed some of the niceties of civilized social life. Or perhaps it was just that, as in other enclosed communities, gossip and rumour became magnified out of all proportion because there was no outside world to dilute it.

The silence seemed to last for a long time. Paula glanced at Eugene, wanting to show that she appreciated his intervention, but he avoided her eye and attacked his roast duck with enthusiasm. Wise of him, thought Paula: he's a lot wiser than I thought at first.

Mercy spoke at last. "I'm sorry, Paula. You've gotten yourself very involved with Josephine and her folks and it must have been a shock to you. It's a bit of a shock to us too, isn't it, Gene?"

He nodded. "Should we send flowers too? Or send a note to Louis? What do you think, Paula?"

"I think the best thing would be just to mention it when you see him," she replied. "I don't think there's any need for anything else, but I'm sure he would be grateful to have it acknowledged and not to have to keep explaining about it himself.''

It sounded even to her own ear as if she was taking a rather proprietorial attitude towards Louis, but the others simply said they thought she was quite right, and let the subject drop at last, having established, largely by some sort of unspoken concensus, the manner in which it was henceforth to be dealt with between them. Social manners had triumphed, and whatever Mercy's reservations, it was unlikely that she would let loose such an attack on Paula again.

Colin arrived as they were eating their dessert. He was quiet and subdued, accepted the Fordhams' commiserations on his mother's accident with very little comment, praised the efficiency of the medical staff, and proceeded to eat in silence.

Paula was glad to leave the table. She went straight down to the cabin, now tidied up and with the bedcover turned down for the night, picked up the books for Julie, and walked down the gold-carpeted stairs and along the starboard corridor to Julie's cabin, glancing at the little side corridor that led to the ship's hospital as she went by, and noting that the main door of the hospital was now closed.

Julie had a cabin very similar to her own. There was a second berth in it which had never been claimed.

''I expected to share,'' she told Paula, ''but apparently the woman cancelled. I was rather pleased about it until I went and crippled myself, but since then I've been thinking that it might have been rather nice if—''

She broke off, probably not wanting to show just how lonely she felt, and thanked Paula for the books and for visiting her.

''It's not entirely out of goodness of heart,'' said Paula, ''and I hope you won't get fed up with me if I come and take refuge with you from time to time. There's people on this ship whom I want to avoid, and you make a wonderful excuse.''

Julie did not, to Paula's relief, enquire who the people were, but chatted a bit about herself. They discovered a mutual interest in long country walks and orienteering, and Paula found her both restful and refreshing, a breath of cool air on an overheated imagination.

But presently Julie said, ''We had quite a bit of excitement at the hospital after they'd fixed my leg and I was waiting for them to wheel me back here. Nurse Lander— you said you'd met her, didn't you?—was sitting with me telling me what I was allowed to do and what I wasn't— she's a bit of a bossyboots but she does know her job— and then in comes this guy without knocking or anything and completely ignores my presence and says he's got to see her urgently.''

''What sort of a guy?'' asked Paula.

''Oh—youngish. Dark beard, pug nose. Medium height. Not particularly appealing, but maybe he had toothache or something. Anyway, our blond friend didn't look any too pleased and I had the impression that she'd already met him and might even know him quite well. He was creating quite a scene, as they say, and there were two other people there waiting for treatment and they looked quite interested and all on the alert. You know how it is when people suspect anybody of going out of line, and this was just the sort of guy who always pushes himself in ahead of everybody else. I don't know what happened next because the receptionist came back and brought me to my cabin.''

''How did he speak?'' asked Paula. ''What sort of accent?''

''Oh, not American or Canadian. Definitely a Brit. Vaguely Northern, I think.''

''Then I'm sure I know him,'' said Paula, making a face of distaste.

"One of those you're trying to avoid?" said Julie laughing.

"That's right. He sits at my table."

"Poor you. Say no more. And be my guest." Julie waved her hand round the little cabin as if offering the freedom of a large mansion. "Whenever you like. I can't thank you enough, Paula. I was dreading the rest of this voyage but feel I can face it now."

"Would you like me to move in with you?" said Paula, suddenly inspired.

"Gosh. Do you really mean it?" There was no doubt about Julie's enthusiasm for the suggestion. "It's not that I can't move at all. I can stagger to the loo and keep myself decently clean. And the stewards are helpful and kind. But it's just . . ."

Again she broke off. She's very young, thought Paula, barely twenty, and it's not much fun being laid up like this among strangers and far from home.

"I'm not offering to nurse you," she said, "but it would be company for us both. For various reasons I'm not very happy with my own cabin."

She hoped she would not be asked the reasons, and once again the admirable Julie did not probe.

"When the night steward comes," she said, "I'll get him to bring the other key to the cabin, and then you can come and go as you like."

"Lovely," said Paula. "I'd better tell my stewards too, and then there's a few things I have to do, but I shan't be very late in coming to bed. See you."

"See you," echoed Julie happily.

— 15 —

But I have not given up my quest, said Paula to herself as she returned slowly and thoughtfully to her own cabin and put together the few things that she needed to take back with her to Julie's. There are still some things that I would like to know about and I also ought perhaps to tell Louis that I am moving out.

She thought for a moment or two and then knocked on the door of Cabin 3033. To leave a note was cowardly. Besides, there were other reasons why she wanted to know if he was in there. If she could get Denis to go in and look for that key . . .

No reply came to her knock. It was not yet ten o'clock, and the great majority of the passengers were enjoying this particularly festive evening in their various ways. Presumably Louis had had his sleep and was working hard at keeping up the pretence that Josephine was still alive. Or perhaps there were more formalities that had to be attended to. How greatly relieved he would be, and also the members of crew involved, when they reached port. The whole business was quite bad enough, even without the added suspicion that it might not have been an accidental death.

When she was away from the cabin Paula felt sure that it was indeed accidental. When she was at the door of No.

152

3033 she began to doubt again. At this moment she was glad that the cabin was empty. She rang the bell for the night steward and Denis appeared immediately.

"Denis," she said before he could say his little piece, "are you very busy?"

"Not yet, ma'am. Not for about another hour. Then they'll all start wanting their nightcaps at once."

"Then would you stay and talk for a while? I'm very anxious to get something straight in my mind and I'm sure you can help. Do sit down. Would you like a cigarette?"

He accepted and sat down, easily and without any embarrassment, in the green chair.

"It's about Mrs. Hillman," she said at last.

A wary look came into his eyes.

"It's all right. I know what's happened," said Paula. "Mr. Hillman told me himself. He said he oughtn't to have done so, but in view of the fact that I was next door and had been rather closely involved . . ."

"Yes, ma'am," said Denis as she paused and did not continue. "Very sad. Very tragic accident. But they do happen sometimes. Particularly in bad weather."

"Have you ever known a fatal accident before?" asked Paula.

"Yes, ma'am, I have," was the reply. "It was a member of crew. But you don't want to hear about that, ma'am. You want me to tell you what happened this morning after you asked me to go in next door."

It was said without any disrespect; purely as a statement of fact.

"Yes," agreed Paula. "That's exactly what I do want, and I'll tell you why, Denis. There seems to be some sort of suggestion being made, in fact it was actually made to me by a passenger, not a member of crew, that it was not purely an accident, but that somebody might have hit her. It's worrying me all the time and I can't stop thinking about it. Is this rumour going round the crew as well?"

"Yes," replied Denis, "but not seriously. I mean nobody really believes it. People always say this sort of thing when something like this happens. Did she fall or was she pushed? You know how it is, ma'am."

"I know how it is," said Paula thoughtfully. "But there's another well-known saying, that there's many a true word spoken in jest."

"Not in this case." Denis was most emphatic. "Sailors are very superstitious. Even people like me who most people don't think of as sailors at all. No one likes deaths at sea, but you always get them on these cruise ships. It's all these old people who think it's such an easy way to travel. It can't be helped, but we don't make jokes about it. Not when it's true. If there'd really been a murder nobody would joke about it. I can promise you that, ma'am."

The boy was looking at her very seriously now, almost with compassion.

"It's a pity you had to get mixed up in it, ma'am," he went on. "Sort of spoilt your trip, you might say."

"It has rather, but it's partly my own fault and one can't think of that after what has happened. After you went into the cabin this morning," continued Paula, prompting him.

"There was Nurse Lander from the hospital. I don't know her well but I know she's a bit of a terror—and Mr. Knight. He's Mrs. Hillman's son, as you no doubt know, ma'am."

"Yes. He sits at our table," said Paula.

"They started going at it hammer and tongs," continued Denis, "he and the nurse, the moment I came in. He wanted Mrs. Hillman to go to hospital, she said there was no need. But they hadn't been talking about that before I came. They'd been talking about something quite different, and talking very friendly together, too. I didn't hear much, but I did hear him say something like 'leaving him everything.' "

" 'Leaving him everything,' " repeated Paula thoughtfully. "What does that suggest to you, Denis?"

"Somebody making a will," he replied promptly.

"It does to me too. And earlier on I'd heard Mrs. Hillman more or less threatening to cut Mr. Knight out of her will. I bet that's it," she went on excitedly, "I bet they were discussing how to stop her making a new will. And he must have found out something more about it, and that's why he was trying to see Nurse Lander at the hospital this evening. I don't know what you must think of me, Denis. I don't usually go poking my nose into other people's business like this. Or if I do, it usually starts with the best of intentions."

"The path to hell is paved with good intentions," said Denis solemnly, and then they both burst out laughing. "I think you're"—he went a little pink in the face and looked younger than ever and sounded suddenly rather shy—"I think you're one of the nicest passengers I've ever had. And a pal of mine has seen Mr. Knight and Nurse Lander together several times," he went on hurriedly, "but neither of them had anything to do with Mrs. Hillman's fall, I'm quite sure of that."

"How can you be sure?"

"Because when I came in I went to the bathroom door and called out to Mrs. Hillman, asking if she needed any help. They couldn't stop me, either of them, because I said she'd rung the bell for the steward. There's bells in the bathroom, ma'am. Perhaps you hadn't noticed."

"Of course," murmured Paula. "Had she really rung?"

"No, but they weren't to know that, were they?" Denis accepted another cigarette before going on. "They were nonplussed, as you might say. I've never used that word before," he added as an aside. "I've always wanted to. I like using words and phrases."

"You're showing off," said Paula reproachfully. "And

you're keeping me on tenterhooks. There's another good word. Do hurry up, Denis.''

"So I called out to Mrs. Hillman and she called back, 'Is that Denis?' And I said, 'Yes, it is.' And she said, 'Don't open the door. Send them away. I don't want to see anybody at all except my husband. I'm not coming out of here till my husband comes. Where is he?' So I promised her I'd locate him at once, but she needn't worry, the others couldn't get in.''

"They must have been furious," said Paula.

"They were that. If looks could kill. I didn't see how they could possibly break into the bathroom but I didn't trust them an inch. So I came into your cabin here, ma'am—taking the liberty, and finding it unlocked—and used your telephone to call around and try to track down Mr. Hillman. And somebody said they'd just seen him getting out of the Midships elevator on Three Deck and I said to myself, Okay, it's up to him now, and went back to the pantry.''

"You didn't actually see him?"

"I saw him when I was in the pantry. He was hurrying along the corridor, getting along like a real seaman, not staggering around like most passengers. He didn't see me, but I thought, that's all right then. He'll sort them all out. And I went off to bed.''

"Of course," said Paula. "You weren't supposed to be on duty at all. And after that effort of yours . . .''

Denis stood up. "I'll have to be going, ma'am. They'll be ringing for me any moment now. Will you be wanting anything here yourself?''

"No, thanks." Paula explained about her move to Julie's cabin. "But I'll see you again," she added. "I want to thank you properly, and if there is anything else at all that I can do for you—''

"There is something, ma'am.''

He looked very shy again and after some careful questioning Paula discovered that he was writing poems and had never dared to show them to anybody, but since she was a teacher of English Literature . . .

"If you'll leave them in here," said Paula, "then I'll have a chance to look at them during the day and tomorrow evening I'll ring and we'll fix a time to talk. I don't know whether I'll be able to help you, but I'll do my best. And, Denis."

"Yes, ma'am?"

"Do you think that Mr. Hillman could have hit or pushed Mrs. Hillman when he went into the bathroom and that was what caused the accident?"

Paula waited in some anxiety for his reply. Of all the people she had become acquainted with on this ship she felt that this young steward was the one whose opinion she would most trust. He seemed to possess a practical common sense and a sense of humour and an imaginative attitude towards his surroundings and towards other people. A good combination of qualities, making for good balance, which was just what was needed on this ship. She was curious to see what sort of poetry he was writing and hoped very much that she would sincerely be able to praise it.

"I guess it would have been physically possible for him to injure or kill his wife," replied Denis slowly. "He could have held her and actually cracked her head down on the edge of the bath. She was feeling very giddy and she trusted him. There wouldn't have been any struggle. It would need quick thinking and quick acting, but he could do it. Only I don't think he did." Denis shook his head. "I can't give you my reasons, ma'am. It's just that I feel he really cared about his wife. Not in any sentimental way. But really cared, just the same. Otherwise—well, ma'am, I'd say he's a very cool customer indeed and the sort who could get away with murder."

"You have taken the words out of my mouth," said Paula.

"Some more flowers for Mrs. Hillman," said the hospital receptionist in a rather despairing voice the following morning. "What on earth are we to do with them?"

"I'll take them," snapped Nurse Lander, "and you'd better be careful what you say, Rosalie."

"But there's nobody here. Only ourselves."

"You can't be too careful."

After Veronica had gone, Rosalie and the nurse whose name was Polly looked at each other and shrugged. Nurse Lander had never been popular with the staff, and she had been worse than ever since Mrs. Hillman's death. The others were quite sure that they knew why. She was trying to get off with the widower, who was a charming and good-looking man and quite a well-known writer, but she wasn't making any headway. The dead woman's son, who did seem to be hanging round her rather a lot, was a very poor substitute.

The rest of the medical staff talked a great deal among themselves and hoped that Nurse Lander would carry out her frequently expressed intention to hand in her notice.

At a table for four in the dining room, Mercy Fordham said: "I guess we won't see Colin until we've nearly finished breakfast. He seems to be avoiding us, and I for one don't care."

"Nor I," said Eugene.

"Nor I," said Paula.

"And I'm going to throw all caution to the winds," said Mercy, "and have eggs sunny side up with my bacon."

"I'm going to have crumpets. That's the same as English muffins, isn't it," said Eugene.

"So am I," said Paula, "with lashings of honey."

The Chinese steward took their orders, bowing his head

slightly as he noted each one, and looking as inscrutable as ever.

"Another classical concert this evening," said Mercy, consulting her programme for the day. "He's an excellent pianist. Do try to come this time, Paula."

"Yes, I'll come," promised Paula.

"How is your friend?" asked Eugene.

"Julie? Much better today. I'm going to try to get her up to the Boat Deck so that she can have some fresh air. It's miserable being down there in the cabin, especially when you don't even feel ill."

"Today's quiz," remarked Eugene, consulting his daily programme, "deals exclusively with the sea and seamanship. I guess we give that one a miss."

"Me too," said Paula. "I shan't be able to answer anything."

"There's a film on the treasures of the Louvre," said Mercy. "I'd like to see that."

They were quite easy and friendly together, the three of them, but it was not as it had been before. Each was too conscious of the things that had to remain unsaid, and Paula was not sorry to leave the table and return to Julie's cabin.

She saw Louis only once that day, when she came to collect the poems that Denis had left in her own cabin. She was in the doorway, holding the folded sheets of handwriting, when Louis came out of Cabin 3033.

It was impossible not to greet each other. Paula explained about Julie.

"Perhaps it's just as well," said Louis. "It will help you both. It hasn't been very pleasant for you, having all this happen next door."

"It's not exactly that," said Paula. "It's that—oh, I must be a most garrulous and indiscreet sort of person, but I do find this secrecy a terrible effort, and it's much easier if I run round after Julie and try to forget it. When I think of what you are having to put up with it makes me feel ashamed of myself.''

''There's no need to worry about me, and I'm delighted that you've found a means of coping with it. The day after tomorrow we'll be in port. The time will soon go.''

Paula could find nothing to say, but neither could she excuse herself and depart. He looked lonely and tired, and she felt an impulse to try to give comfort which conflicted with her own sense of self-protection. With the Fordhams it had been possible to draw back from the brink of too great and too sudden an exchange of confidences, and return to a normal acquaintanceship. But with Louis there was no going back. It was all or nothing.

The ''all'' would be to go right behind the scenes, to see what lay behind the mask of the actor, to get to the heart of the mystery. For the sense of mystery about him was as strong as ever, stronger, perhaps, since Josephine's death and since Paula's conversation with Denis. Her fascination with mystery was very great indeed, but on this occasion it seemed to be fighting a losing battle with her apprehension.

It would have to be nothing. There was no way to get back to any sort of rewarding relationship after all that had taken place.

Yet it was very hard just to go away. In her perplexity Paula found she was turning over and over in her hands the manuscript sheets of Denis' poems, and Louis remarked on them.

''Somebody asked me to read something they'd written,'' she explained. ''I'm hoping I can say something nice about it.''

''As you did to me.'' He smiled briefly but very sweetly. ''I shall treasure that evening.''

''So shall I,'' said Paula, ''and I still can't help wishing—''

''That you could read the whole manuscript?''

"Yes. I wish you would change your mind. If it was largely because of Josephine—"

Paula broke off again, scolding herself for her own incoherence and yet at the same time conscious of a great quickening of interest, as if something very important was taking place.

"It was largely because of Josephine and I have changed my mind," said Louis. "I will send you the typescript when we get back to England. Where shall I address it?"

"To college would be best," replied Paula. "There's always somebody there to take in a parcel. But I'll give you my home address too," she added, conscious that to withhold it could imply a lack of trust. It was typical of her whole attitude towards Louis Hillman. On the one hand was this suspicion that he was not what he seemed, this strong sense of mystery, almost of fear. But at the same time she had the impression of a deeply lonely and unhappy human being aching for the comfort of human companionship.

Perhaps the manuscript would provide the clue. She was excited at the thought of reading it, glad that they were to maintain this contact. It would be quite different when they were both back in England, immersed in their normal lives and activities, instead of being shut up in the artificial hot-house atmosphere of this floating luxury hotel.

He produced a card and she took it and then dictated her address in Hampstead for him to write in his diary. "But please send the parcel to me at work," she added. "Truly it would be safer, and I am so grateful that you are entrusting me with it. I'll take great care. I seem to be rather disorderly, I know, but when it comes to essentials I am always careful. Truly I am."

"I believe you, Paula. Otherwise I wouldn't be letting you have the manuscript at all."

They had moved into Cabin 3033 as they were speaking

and were now seated, Paula in the chair, Louis on Josephine's bed.

"May I comment on it?" asked Paula. "May I suggest a publisher? Although you'll know much more about that than I do," she hastily added.

"I'll look forward to receiving your comments," he said, "but I don't think there is any question of suggesting a publisher. When you have read it you will understand why. Shall we have a goodbye drink together? Tomorrow evening—the last evening—in the Jacobean Bar?"

"I'd like that very much," said Paula.

"Half-past nine, then?"

"Half-past nine."

She was pleased that he had suggested this meeting, grateful to him for achieving what she herself had been unable to. They would talk as shipboard acquaintances about the affairs of the ship, loosening the spring, unwinding the tension that had arisen between them. And in the near future there was the promise of that manuscript, about which she now had a curiosity even greater than before.

"So long for now then," she said, standing up.

"See you," he replied.

And she came out of Cabin 3033, for the last time, without a backward glance, but with an impression of intolerable sadness, an impression of a human being isolated from his fellows as surely as the *Gloriana* was isolated by the sea.

EPILOGUE

Paula went straight from Richard's flat in Bloomsbury to her room at College. She was glad that he had not been able to meet the ship at Southampton and that their meeting had been delayed for several days because of an unexpected assignment of his in Paris.

The reunion had been a mixture of joy and pain for them both. There had been no need to say anything: he had guessed at once what the answer was going to be and had simply said: "Then we go on as before. As we decided."

After that they had talked and talked, both bursting with things they wanted to tell each other, jumping easily from one subject to another, neither monopolizing the conversation.

It had seemed to be all right, but it was not. There was a great ache of disappointment on one side, a great gulf of despair on the other. Paula came away, after they had arranged to spend the weekend together, wishing with all her heart that she knew herself less well. With a little more self-deception she would have jumped impulsively into another big mistake, another marriage that could not possibly last.

But they would have been happy for a while, argued one half of her mind.

Which would have made the painful parting all the worse
when it came, argued the other.

The argument continued, but it was the second voice
that always came out on top, bringing with it the same
overwhelming sense of loss that she had experienced when
she sat in limbo on the Boat Deck of the *Gloriana*. Only
this time there was no Louis to pull her out of it into what,
from this distance, seemed to have been a magical evening.

Term started next week and there was a little pile of
mail on her desk. She glanced through it without much
interest, decided that there was nothing urgent, and was
about to leave when the telephone rang. It was the porter's
lodge to say that they had a registered parcel for her, and
would she like to collect it?

It was a brown paper parcel, very neat and with the
typed label addressed to Dr. Paula Glenning at the Department of English Language and Literature. There was
hardly any need to glance at the name of the sender: she
knew instantly that this was Louis' manuscript and that
he must have sent it off very soon after he got home. She
gripped it tightly as she waited for the Hampstead bus,
and when she got off she hesitated for a moment. It was
a beautiful late September day, with promise of several
more hours of sunshine. Should she find a quiet spot on
the Heath and sit and read it there? She loved to sit on the
grass under an oak tree, feeling very much in the country-
side but with the wide distant panorama of London spread
out in front of her.

In the end she decided to go home. This manuscript was
very precious and it would be safer indoors.

The big attic room was as untidy as ever. The efforts to
live up to Richard's standards of perfection had been aban-
doned before she left for the States. But she unwrapped
the parcel with care instead of tearing at it impatiently.
Inside were about two hundred pages of typescript, with

occasional insertions and excisions, held together by a light
loose folder and a couple of rubber bands.

There was also a long envelope on which was written a
message in the handwriting that had so intrigued Mercy
Fordham.

"Dear Paula, here is the script, and in this envelope is
a letter, but please do not read it until you have read the
story. When you have finished it, you will see the reason
for the request. Thank you. L."

"All right," said Paula aloud to herself as she put the
envelope to one side. "I won't open it yet. In two or three
hours' time maybe."

She was a quick reader, often taking in the meaning of
a sentence with a kind of gulp of the eyes, but on this
occasion she was going to read more slowly. Three hours
at the outside, with perhaps a break for coffee. But no
cigarettes. This was an only copy, and she was not going
to take the slightest risk of doing any damage to it.

Two and three-quarter hours later, without having
stopped for coffee and without having felt the slightest
urge to light a cigarette, Paula put down the last page and
shuffled the typescript together. She stared at her own familiar walls and window as if coming out of a dream so
vivid that the waking life had no reality.

Still in the dream, she picked up the long envelope and
opened it. It contained several pages of the flowing handwriting and read as follows: "Dear Paula,

"You are now the only other person in the world who
knows the story of Heinrich Fliess, whose friend Ludwig
was drowned in the sea a few miles from Dover on a
stormy night nearly fifty years ago.

"Yes, I can see in my mind's eye the amazement and
disbelief in your sweet face, but it is a true story that you
have just read, not in every detail, but in its essence. Ludwig and I were both orphans. That was not unusual at that
time in the part of the world where we lived, and that was

one of the reasons why we were accepted on the children's
refugee transport. It was ill-organized, and there was much
confusion and overcrowding, both on the train and on the
boat. There was nobody else from our home village; nobody who knew either of us.

"When the alarm went up that fire had broken out, the
panic broke all bounds. Children fought and screamed and
struggled to get to the rail of the ship, to the lifeboats, to
where the lifebelts hung. And by the time it proved to be
a false alarm, a boy had gone overboard in the turmoil.

"It was Ludwig, and I ought to have found our leader
and told him and asked for the ship to turn back and
search, but I did not do so. I don't know why. I think I
was paralyzed, as in a nightmare. It was all a nightmare.

"When we got to Dover I carried his things off as well
as my own. We both had very little. Nobody counted us
or checked that all were there. Nobody mentioned that
there was anyone missing. I suppose the other children
who had noticed it were too frightened to say.

"And nobody knew my name, nor bothered to ask.

"It was when we were told that the arrangements that
had been made for us in England were in fact not made at
all that I first had the idea. I knew that Ludwig had distant
relations in Canada who had never seen him. He had told
me about them, shown me the notebook in which he had
written their address, and which he kept, together with
personal mementoes and documents of importance, in the
little briefcase that was now in my possession. I had no
such connections, neither in Canada nor in any other part
of the world except my own homeland.

"The camp at Dover was full of rumours. Nobody knew
what was going to happen to those unfortunate children
who had nobody. They might even be sent back, to what
sort of fate the world has long since been fully aware. But
in those times anything was possible, and I made my decision. It was to be Heinrich Fliess who had fallen over-

board: Ludwig Bergmann would go to Canada. We were the same height and build and not unlike each other in appearance, and the photographs on our travel documents were very blurred.

"I think that is all I need to say about my manuscript. You will have learned from the story—the story of my life—just what sort of a life the impersonator is condemned to lead. It is a hell of loneliness. I had to write this book, otherwise I could not have survived. And I had to let Josephine see it. There was no way I could write anything without her knowing.

"And she guessed.

"You may think that gave her such a hold over me that I killed her to break loose. But that is not the case. I did deeply resent her control over my writing, and often I longed to be free, but oddly enough it was a relief to know that she knew my secret, and after her death—which has now been recorded as accidental—I found the burden of my loneliness so intolerable that I decided to send you my book to read.

"You had asked to read it; you had already broken down a part of the barrier. I very nearly told you that evening on the Boat Deck when I quoted some of it to you. In telling you the context of the quotation I even mentioned that I had called the main character Henry, after my only friend.

"I think I half hoped that you might, as Josephine had done, guess the truth. But how could you do so, with so little evidence? All it did was to puzzle you and awaken your curiosity. I wanted you to know, but I had acted so much that I could not stop acting. Had we been able to talk again as we talked that evening, then I would have told you what I am writing in this letter. But the storm blew up, and Josephine was seasick. And Josephine and I quarrelled yet again, not about me but about Colin—she wanted to cut him completely out of her will—she was

always making new wills—and I said that would mean he'd
be hanging round me forever and she'd better make it fifty-
fifty. . . . It was a ridiculous quarrel, one of those stupid
things that blow up out of all proportion when there is
already tension between two people.

"And Colin got Veronica Lander to try to help him
prevent his mother from making a new will, presumably
promising her a share. But of course none of us had the
least notion that she was so soon to die. And the rest of
the stupid muddle you know yourself.

"I didn't love her but she was very important to me,
and I miss her very badly indeed. I am particularly sorry
that our last words together were so little worth remembering.

"And now I must await the comments that you promised to send me when you return the manuscript. I am as
anxious as a very raw young author awaiting the verdict
of his first literary offering. I hope to hear from you soon.
I hope your own dilemma has resolved itself without too
great distress.

"What shall I sign myself? I think I will leave it to you
to choose in what manner you will address your friend and
admirer . . ."

The letter finished with a large question mark. Paula sat
staring at it, half in and half out of her dream. Had the
book been by a writer unknown to her she would have felt
much the same. It was one of the most haunting stories
she had ever read. The mystery of the Henry of the book,
as of the real Heinrich, resolved itself only gradually,
piecemeal, and was not fully revealed until the end. It was
a first-class exercise in suspense as well as being a deeply
disturbing study of the human spirit.

But the Henry in the book had let his friend fall to his
death without trying to save him. Paula could actually feel
herself on the tossing little ferry boat, with the rain and
the spray soaking the crowded deck, and the smell of salt

and of tar, and of fear as well; and the shrieks of the children, eerie as wounded animals, and the tumult of their desperate pushing and scrambling.

Perhaps the real Heinrich had indeed helped to push his friend Ludwig overboard, albeit unwillingly, unwittingly. Anything was possible in those circumstances. It was also very possible that the man she had known on the *Gloriana* did not himself know exactly what had happened on that sea trip so long ago. That there was any malice towards his friend was out of the question. The loss must have been stunning. Only later, when it once again became a question of sheer survival, did Heinrich take the step that condemned him to a life sentence of a lie.

Paula folded the letter and replaced the sheets in the long envelope. Then she put the manuscript back in its wrapping paper, making as neat a parcel of it as she could, and placed it on her desk. The glow of the western sky was still visible through the dormer window and she decided to have a short walk on the Heath, followed by something to eat and drink, before she wrote her own letter. The process of returning fully to her own identity after the reading of a book or the hearing of a play was taking much longer than usual.

But when she eventually sat down in her favourite armchair and took up a ball-point pen and a writing pad, she wrote only one word before she came to a stop.

"Dear—"

What should she call him now? How would he like to be addressed, who did he feel himself to be? She tried to imagine herself in a similar situation and decided that she would like to be called by the name she was first known by, her own original name.

"Dear Heinrich," she wrote, and instantly decided that it looked quite wrong. Even if he had continued to live as himself, he would have long since adopted the English version of his name.

Paula tore up the page and wrote "Dear Henry" at the head of the next one. This looked wrong too. It was as if she was writing to a stranger. Or to a character in a book. She swore as she crumpled up this second sheet of paper, and muttered to herself, "What's in a name indeed."

At last, after a lot more thought, she wrote:

"My dear friend 'Louis Hillman,' I think it might be best to publish this manuscript under a different pen name, since it is of such an entirely different quality from those you have published up till now. I have one or two minor comments, and I would rather put them to you in person than write them down. Would you like to meet me at College? We can have lunch there and discuss it in comfort. I do hope you can make it soon, and I will do my best to tell you just what an impression the manuscript made on me. Of course it has got to be published. There is no earthly reason why not. Nobody needs to know that it is your own story, and even if they did, it would not matter. You have done nothing wrong, committed no crime . . ."

Paula's pen flowed on. It was easy to write, now that she had found the right tone, the right relationship. She was addressing a writer, somebody who had something worthwhile to say and an original manner of saying it, and her job as a teacher and champion of English literature was to make sure that other people had a chance of reading it too.

Anna Clarke was born in Cape Town and educated in Montreal and Oxford. She holds degrees in economics and English literature and has held a wide variety of jobs, mostly in publishing and university administration. She is the author of eighteen previous novels, including *Last Judgement*, *Soon She Must Die*, *We the Bereaved*, and *Letter From the Dead*, published by the Crime Club.